i

Baseball Magic

Jay Martin

Pocol Press

POCOL PRESS
Published in the United States of America
by Pocol Press
6023 Pocol Drive
Clifton, VA 20124
www.pocolpress.com

Publisher's Cataloguing-in-Publication

Martin, Jay.

    Baseball magic / Jay Martin. – 1st ed. – Clifton, VA : Pocol Press, 2008.

       p. ; cm.

       ISBN: 978-1-929763-35-1

       1. Baseball--United States--Fiction.
    2. Baseball stories. I. Title.

    PS3563.A724333 B37 2008
    813.6–dc22   0803

DEDICATION

Affectionately
dedicated to
my brother
S. Charles Martin
my first and only coach

TABLE OF CONTENTS

BASEBALL MAGIC

Francisco Platon hovers over his locker. He is hiding something. But he's also anxious to show it to a select audience.

I wander over. He lets me look. His locker is jam-packed.

From it he takes out something wrapped in a towel. For all I know it could be a polished rhinoceros skull. I won't be surprised if he reaches into it and pulls out a bloody shrunken head by the hair.

This guy is like that. He's from Haiti. We have two Haitian baseball players on our team. They came in a package deal. They talk together. His friend, Francisco Broulee, is standing in the little group. His eyes are bulging, big and white.

It's just a baseball.

"What's the big deal?" someone asks.

"It's *the* ball," Platon whispers.

"*The* ball?"

"Sure," he says. "I paid fifty dollars for it."

"There's plenty of balls in the stadium," I mention. "All you want. Fifty dollars?"

"This," he says, beaming, showing his teeth, "is the ball that Meester Romero hit into the stands in the ninth last night. The home run ball. Won the game for them."

"So? You want a souvenir?" Rog asks. "What'd we want it for?"

"To destroy it," Platon says. Broulee shakes his head in vigorous agreement.

Platon pulls a little vise out of his locker and fastens it to the bench he's sitting on.

Next comes a saw. He begins surgery.

"What are you doing?" I inquire.

I feel a little nuts, like he is, even asking this.

"Cutting into pieces."

Broulee explains: "Last night was the first game of the three game series. They had the luck, hit a home run to win the game."

"Yes," Platon interrupts. "This has their good luck in it. We cut it up, the luck goes out."

"Then," Broulee says, "it comes to us. We win the next two games. That's the way."

"Is that how you do it?" Rog says in disgust. "The way I thought it was, you had a pitcher who could pitch. The batters get some hits. We get some runs, they get fewer. That's how I thought it was."

1

"Certainly," Platon says, "but we get the hits because we got the luck. How else we get hits, huh?"

Why argue? He cuts the ball up, gives each of us a piece and goes to the other guys in the locker room who weren't watching. "Have a piece," he says. "Put it in your locker. Tonight put in your back right pocket when you bat. Left pocket for the pitchers. We're winning now, sure."

I take mine. I eye the trashcan. Platon and Broulee will go crazy if I toss it. Maybe we'd have to have a ju-ju ceremony that would last an hour and involve pricking our fingers to get some blood. Maybe he has a live chicken stuffed into his locker. I put my little piece of the magic baseball into my locker, on the top shelf. Maybe he'd object if I put it right on the bottom with my shoes.

Roger does the same. We think alike. We've been playing ball together for a couple of years in the minors, Triple A. Now, we're in Mexico playing winter league for the Vera Cruz Bandits. Maybe that's bad luck too. It will be bad luck for us if we don't get picked up by some big league team soon.

Our team. Assorted Mexicans, the Haitian twins, a utility infielder from the Dominican Republic, a guy who grew up in Spanish Harlem, a Jew, and even a Chinese catcher named Sam Wing, who was born in Fujien province and emigrated with his family to San Bruno, California. You'd think that he at least would not be into voodoo. But he grabs the piece of baseball that Broulee gives him as if it is a treasure and throws it into a red silk bag. Once he showed me what he has in there, some of it anyway – two old coins with square holes in the middle. A little bone, maybe the shin bone of a rodent or else his grandmother's thumb bone, for all I know. The mummified head of a snake. A tin whistle, and whatnot. He let me in on the news that I was a special friend of his. I'm really honored, you know, just so long as I don't have to finger a moldy snake's head. Now he's got a piece of lucky baseball in his bag too. We'll never lose a game again.

I've seen this sort of mumbo jumbo before. When we lose, then they say: the moon has changed. The opposing team got new magic or someone on the other side has an even more moldy snake head. Or one of the Mexican players on the other team paid a witch doctor or a curandero to put a curse on us. That's why they won. Bad Feng Shui. That kind of thing.

More trouble. Our manager, Raphael Guiterrez, comes in with a new player. He's a Cuban who defected when the Fidels were playing

2

in Costa Rica. An outfielder. We need one bad, one who hits. They say he hits. A lot of those Cuban players could go right into the majors. They say he could do it.

He looks it too. He's tall, six-six at least and powerfully built, with thick hairy arms that hang out of the sleeves of the new Hawaiian shirt they gave him. His forearms are like hams in an Ozark smokehouse.

"This is Henry Mungo." Raphael introduces him around. "Henry Mungo is playing in centerfield tonight." Moon Majestic, who's been our centerfielder, goes slinking off to the john.

My name is Henry too. Henry Rogers, the All-American boy. I wonder: will the Francisco boys think it is bad luck to have two Henry's on the team? Or maybe good luck? I hope it's good. I don't want to see Platon start putting one of the Henrys in a vise and making small ones out of a big one. Especially if it is me. I wouldn't put it past him.

Henry Mungo, though, looks very pleased. He shakes hands all around. Is it lucky to shake hands with a Cuban? I can't get this lucky thing out of my mind. Raphael says to him as Mungo pokes out his sweaty hand to me, "Henry Mungo, this is Henry Rogers." He is really happy. "Henry – we be comrades sure," he says, and gives me a goofy grin. He sure has a mouthful of gorgeous teeth and bright red gums. The bathroom where he's been brushing his teeth must have good Feng Shui.

He speaks English too.

He explains that his father was a professor of languages at the university. Now Dad is a cab driver so he can make decent money. In Cuba, professors make almost the same as street sweepers. But a taxi driver who deals with foreign tourists can get his hands on hard currency.

When he shakes with Platon and Broulee he jabbers in their, as we say, *patois*. As it turns out he speaks French, Creole, Spanish, Portuguese, and, of course, Russian. I half expect him to address Sam Wing in Mandarin too, except that Sam doesn't know a word of Mandarin, only some strange dialect from Fujien and what passes for English in San Bruno.

"You'll bunk with Moon," Raphael says. That's all right with Henry. They're both centerfielders.

I'm lucky. It's a well-known fact that Rog and I are roomies.

Of course, our girlfriends are down here too, and Rog and I don't sleep in the team rooms much. We go over to the girls' hotel every night and spend all day at the pool until it's time for a game. At night the girls come to watch us play.

3

Most of the teams in the winter league have some Americans on them. Not from the majors, of course, but guys like us who usually bat between .250 and.275. In Vera Cruz we look like major players, and we may get to hit over .300 here. A few scouts from U.S. teams come down, and if we look good we might catch on with a big league team. Stateside, Rog and I worked our way up to Triple A. Now it's the majors or washout, down the alphabet.

Platon gives Mungo a piece of the baseball.

"Thanks a lot, I'm really grateful," Henry says, pumping Platon's and then Broulee's hands.

Sid Sloan, our third baseman, comes up next to me and says: "I don't like the looks of that guy." I think he means Mungo, but he could mean almost anybody except Roger and me. We're in his good books. He used to play for the Phillies, but he's been washed up for years now and just plays winter ball. Everybody else on the team looks weird to him. He's probably right. Roger and I are probably weird too, but he just hasn't noticed.

"What's up Sid?"

"Guiterrez" – Sid won't call him Raphael the way the rest of us do – "Guiterrez, it looks like he sold Wally out to the devil to get this Cuban on the team."

Wally was Moon Majestic's roommate – that is, until last week when a horse kicked him in the groin, then trampled on him. He's now in the Vera Cruz hospital and through for the season. Probably any season.

"What do you mean, 'sold him to the devil'?"

"I've got my eye on Guiterrez. He's got a pact with the devil. The old Sly One's got enough on Guiterrez to take him down to the satanic steam room right now. But Guiterrez is a wise one too. He makes trades with the devil. 'Take Wally Dent,' Guiterrez tells the Slitherer, 'instead of me. You can have him in a trade.' Guiterrez gives losers up to the Fiendish Fryer to keep the One-with-the-Forked-Tail from getting to him. It's like throwing scraps of meat to a pack of wild dogs, so they won't turn on you. Only we're the meat."

It was hard to tell if Sid was kidding or has really cracked up. You know, people do snap in foreign countries.

Sid continues: "Sure, remember when we first came down. There was that catcher named Camperstino, Camperoglio, what's his name, in the bloom of life. Guiterrez was looking beaten, all washed out, and the team was losing. Then all of a sudden Campersino falls off a balcony in

4

Merida. It's the first floor balcony. Still, he breaks his neck. Guiterrez gave him to the Evil One. Raphael's looked pretty shipshape ever since."

"And we started winning right after. But wasn't that because you and me and Roger were hitting?" I asked.

"Maybe so. But what about Wally? Why'd he get on a horse? He never rode a horse in his life. I bet Guiterrez, says to him, 'Wally, you need to relax. Take a horseback ride. It'll do you a world of good.' He had it all set up with the Horned Reaper. You'll see. If Wally dies. Guiterrez will look fresh as a daisy."

Platon is sacrificing baseballs, Broulee is spitting over his left shoulder, and Sid is nuts about the devil and Raphael Guiterrez. Me, I'm trying to hit for over .300, that's all. Sure I wish I had a magic spell that would make that happen as easy as abracadabra, but the only way I can do it is to keep my eye on the ball, be patient, don't press, wait them out, play it smart, scatter the hits. All the stuff we were taught in Little League but usually forget.

That night Rog starts hitting. Really hitting. He's four for five, with two home runs. Still, after the game he's got that worried look on his face. We slump down on the locker room benches facing each other.

I say, "What's the hangdog look for? Five for five is the only thing that would make you happy?"

He has a harried look in his eye.

"I've got to keep it up," he says. "I had a telegram waiting for me at the hotel. It says I've been cut. I'm a free agent."

This is bad news about Rog. When you've been playing for only two-three years and you start going down the ladder instead of up, you've had your chance. The game is up – you're twenty-six now, and younger players are going to get their shot. You'll never get into the majors.

I worry about that too. It's not impossible. A couple of years ago we were the young guys. Now I could get a telegram any day too. I hit a few points lower than Roger. But he's an outfielder and should hit for power. Whereas I'm a second baseman with a pretty good glove and a lot of speed. I don't have to hit as high. So I'm not getting telegrams. Not yet.

"I hear a rumor there's a scout coming down here from the Orioles," Rog says. "They need a backup outfielder, don't they? I've got to be hitting when he comes."

"So hit. You did great tonight. When's he coming?"

"That's the trouble. No one knows. Maybe he'll just pop in to see me."

"Maybe he'll come to see Henry Mungo," I say, "and then he'll see you anyway."

"Good."

Rog likes the idea of how all the angles can work for him.

"Yeah, good," he repeats. "Yeah, Mungo hit a long homer tonight, didn't he? And he's only – what? – nineteen, twenty? They'll want a look-see at him. No doubt about it. But I'm hot too. I'm really swinging."

"You'll keep it going," I reassure him.

"I'm racking my brains."

"What for?" I ask.

"To remember everything."

"Like what?"

"Everything. Like what time I got up today. What I had for breakfast. Did I turn on the television in the room? What program? That sort of thing."

"What's it matter?" I wonder.

"It's luck. It's in the stars, it's that when you do everything in a certain way and then you get four out of five, you should do it that way again."

I kid him.

"That's an old time baseball superstition. Besides, maybe you got the benefit of Platon slicing up that baseball. We won, didn't we? All the leftover voodoo got into your bat. Do you have your little piece of the ball?"

As I say, I'm just kidding him, trying to get him to snap out of it. But he takes it to heart.

"I better check," he answers with a straight face, and he rustles on the top shelf of his locker and comes out with it. He has a relieved smile too.

"Here it is. Right. Thanks. I want to put it where I can find it."

He places it in the very center of the shelf.

"Let's get going," I say, "The girls are waiting for us. We'll surely have bad luck if we keep them waiting."

"That's right, that's right. Yeah, we don't want to rock the boat."

Betsy and my girl Monica are sitting in the Cantina.

I don't know if Monica's my girl exactly. I met her back in the States just before the season was over. Rog was already planning to

6

have Betsy come down with him. The four of us double-dated. Monica and Betsy seemed to get along. So, when I said to Monica, "Have you ever been to Mexico?" she answered, "No, do you want to take me!" "Fine with me," I say. It's a good thing she's here too. Betsy would have been lonely without Monica around. And if she were bitchy, that wouldn't do much for Rog's game.

They're drinking Tequila Sunrises. "Sit down," they tell us. "Have something while we finish our drinks. This is a swell Cantina." They want to talk like Hemingway.

It was a pretty nice place too, for Vera Cruz.

"I'll have a beer," I say. "Cerveza, por favor."

"Nothing for me," Rog tells the waiter. "I've got to keep fit."

"You were fit tonight, baby," Betsy remarks. "Two home runs. Let me feel your muscles."

She reaches over playfully to squeeze Rog's arm.

We chit chat about this and that. We won the game ten to four. I got two good singles. Batting .306 now. I'm happy. The girls spent the late afternoon at the local zoo. They have a high time laughing about the animals. Something about the monkey cage was so funny it breaks them up again, but I never find out what the chimps were up to.

It's not long before Rog says, "Let's call it a day."

It's late enough to call it a day, so no one objects. But Roger does seem kind of insistent about it.

Rog's hitting continues without a letup. But every time he raises his batting average by five points he looks more exhausted. Every home run that he hits enlarges the bags under his eyes. He's becoming haggard. Dropped ten pounds maybe. He comes up to the plate every time with a fierce look on his face, and he swings with the abandon of a gladiator with a broadaxe.

Before every game he asks, "Where's that scout for the Orioles? What do they want, blood? I'm hitting .375 already." Our team's in second place.

One evening, with a kind of desperation Rog asks me for reassurance: "You think he'll be here tonight, don't you?"

"Sure. Can't imagine what's keeping him." Roger's getting all the play in the Vera Cruz sports pages.

Rog starts to say wild things like, "I don't know how long I can hold out."

The trouble is, he and Betsy are fighting all the time. One day she says, "I'm not coming to the game tonight."

7

Roger goes wild. He bangs his fist on the table and yells, "Like hell you're not coming. You're coming to the game, that's that."

"Or what?" She answers in a really snotty way. Like, "Make me."

Roger sees he has to make it up to her. "Come on Betsy, you're my girl. You know it's important to me. Do it for me, baby."

He looks like he'll kill himself right there if she says no.

"Well, if you're nice about it," she agrees, and he brightens up.

Meanwhile, the Francisco boys are collecting balls. Every time we win a game, and we're winning most of them now, they try to get the ball that makes the last out. Sometimes they don't get it when an opposing player has the ball in his mitt and won't give it up. They plead with him, and mostly – what the hell – the guy tosses the ball to them. But when they don't get it, they're in a sweat. They do magic with some other ball. They add it to their collection. They've got a dozen or more balls in a crate with all sorts of holy roller pictures painted on it, Christ on the cross, angels and flames, devils. They put a latch and a padlock on it, and they look in it before each game and roll the balls around as if they are reading tea leaves. Wing's red purse looks more full than ever. Probably has a whole snake stuffed into it. He asks if he can put it in the box and the boys are pleased.

Henry Mungo is having a big season. He's keeping up with Rog in the hitting department. Every time Rog, who's batting third, doesn't get a hit, but Henry, who follows him, does, Rog looks sour.

The difference is, where Rog is looking worse with each hit, Henry is getting fatter and healthier looking. Pretty soon he could pose for a magazine like *Health and Fitness*. He's *sleek* – that's the word for it. His hair is growing long and thick, his skin is as creamy and juicy as a potato soup, his long hairy arms look like King Kong's. Pretty soon the newspapers will be calling him "King Kong Mungo."

We've got a good winning streak going and the players are happy.

The only fly in the ointment is Moon Majestic. Bad as Roger seems, Moon is worse. He walks around dazed. He's benched, doesn't even pinch hit. He doesn't care. He just sits in the corner of the dugout and sulks. He's going nowhere in this game. He's getting thinner and thinner.

Henry Mungo, his roomie, is always around, trying to cheer him up, but it does no good.

Sid gets me in a corner of the john when nobody else is in there and fixes me with steely eyes, like in that poem about the Ancient Mariner. "Guiterrez must have done something really bad, and the Cloven-Foot-

8

Man was close to nabbing him. But Guiterrez has thrown Moon to the Wily One, don't you think? He'll take Moon soon. Poof. You'll have seen the last of him. Then the Old Fox will be after Guiterrez again, and Guiterrez'll have to find another piece of fresh meat to throw to the Old Black Dog."

"Kidding, same as ever," I say.

"Not for a minute. I'm confiding in you. You've got to protect yourself. Look what I've got." He fishes something out of his pocket and opens his hand, palm up.

There are six little aluminum crosses there.

"I got them at the mercardo. Take one."

"That's taking the joke too far," I say.

"Take one, take one anyway."

He drops a cross into my shirt pocket.

"Pin it inside your shirt or tuck it in your jock. It can't do any harm, can it? You could be next. It's not going to be me. I'm not going to be the one to save Guiterrez from the Eater of Darkness."

I give him a disgusted look, as if to say "That's enough of this devil bullshit. It's wearing thin."

He pays no attention.

"He's all over Mexico. You can hardly go into a Farmacia without seeing a picture of the Ominous One somewhere. Don'cha know, in Mexico the Ravenous One is more powerful than he is back in the US of A. It's in the air here. They still believe in him here, where back home they don't even think about him anymore, not even on Hallowe'en. We just got masks of Michael Jackson and Al Gore then. Don't take any chances. Put one in your shoe. Look at this."

He lifts up his foot. In the space between the heel and the sole he has nailed a holy medal.

"I'm protected no matter where I walk," he says.

Maybe he has really gone over the edge, I think.

"Okay, Sid," I say, "I'll carry one on me. Thanks for the thought."

"That's good. See that you do. You're looking a little pale. You could be next."

Later, I look into a mirror. I'm getting crazy too. But I don't look pale at all. I'm suntanned a nice brown.

Still, I slip the cross into my back pocket.

"Betsy is really getting me down," Monica says that might. "I don't know if I can stand her much longer. Complain, complain, complain."

"About Rog." I don't even ask it as a question.

9

"What else? What a demanding guy he is. She has to do everything he says, just the way he says to do it. She doesn't have a life of her own."

"What's going on?"

"She doesn't say, not exactly, just: 'the same-old-same-old,' that's all. I'm getting sick and tired."

"Bad news," I say. I feel almost as glum as Moon Majestic looks.

We win eighteen out of twenty-two games. The box of sacred balls that the Franciscos are accumulating is filled. They come in with a bigger box, with even more painting on it, and start a second collection. When we lose, they take the losing ball and pour hot black tar or gooey salve over it. I think they pee on them. I don't want to know what else.

I notice that both Platon and Broulee are wearing little crosses hanging from their left ears. They come in early before games now and burn palm leaves in front of the scoreboard. They wave the smoke toward the scoreboard with a buzzard's feather.

I say, "What's that for?"

They tell me, "We're exorcising the scoreboard. We get the score now. You see."

Next, Monica says to me, "I'm not happy. I'm wasting my time with you. You don't love me at all. I could be back in the States finding a guy who would really be wild about me."

The truth is, I don't really love her that much – I mean we're not Romeo and Juliet, are we? When I think that, I realize that even Shakespeare's play is about some kind of bad luck or fate. There's no way to escape it. Platon and Broulee and even Sid and maybe Rog and Shakespeare are all so convinced that there's some magical method to the madness of the cosmos that I must be the one who's out of step. Maybe I'd be batting more than .309 now if I could find some sort of wacky thing to do. Maybe I could soak my batting glove in a Tequila Sunrise while reading the *Baseball Digest* to it.

But – don't ask me why – I don't want Monica to leave. Bingo, it comes to me out of the blue. She'd stay if I gave her a love potion. I'll ask Raphael. I bet they even have them in the Farmacias here.

"That's easy," Raphael says, "women buy them everyday. Not many Mexican guys do, because there are always plenty of women sniffing around. As soon as there's an aroma in the air that your woman is leaving you, two or three other senoritas will be camping on your doorstep. Why bother importing women when there are thousands of them already down here?"

"Monica suits me," I say.

I express my concern to Sid. He looks worried. "I wouldn't do it," he tells me. "This is a sure way for Guiterrez and the Hunter of Souls to get you in their grip. They'll be something in the love potion that will get a hold of you too."

The next night I tell Raphael, "Forget it about the love potion. I'll just be extra nice."

"I already have it," he says with a toothy grin. "Here it is."

He produces a folded up piece of gray paper. On it a mess of unreadable words are scribbled in watery ink.

Somehow I'd thought that a love potion would come in a little flask, maybe even with a worm in it, like Mezcal. But how do I get her to swallow a piece of paper?

"Put it under the pillow, or even the mattress, and the message will leave the paper and get into her head while she's sleeping. You won't be able to read it in the morning – it will be in her heart."

"I can't read it now," I say.

He gives me a hopeless look. "You're lost, man, if you don't just believe."

I try it. But I don't see a change in Monica the next morning. Maybe it would have worked better if I had kissed her a little before we went to sleep.

"Oh, I guess it's not you, it's Betsy," she says.

This is an improvement. The potion is working.

"I don't blame her," Monica says. "You know what's going on? It's one of those stupid superstitions. Rog says that everyone knows when you're on a hitting streak you got to do the same thing every day, or else you'll break the streak. Ever since three weeks ago, when he hit those two homers and went four for five, he's made a checklist of what he did that day and he's fanatical about following it. He has to eat huevos rancheros with flour tortillas for breakfast every morning. Even Betsy has to do what she did that day. At breakfast she ate grapefruit with coffee. She has to eat the same thing every morning. 'Now' she groans, 'when I look down at a half grapefruit, it looks back at me. That maraschino cherry in the center looks like the eye of a corpse, all bloodshot. God, Rog is wearing the same underwear for the last twenty days. I have to rinse it out every night and hope it dries by morning. Everything has to be the same.' But that's not the worst."

"What is?"

"She says she's not ready to tell me yet." What she does say is that at first for her and Rog it was a ball – like Christmas every day, a big party. But when Christmas has to come every day, day after day, it wears thin. When you have to pluck the same presents off the tree every day and sing the same carols, pretty soon you're sick of it all. 'Christmas every day is for the vultures,' she says, referring to the Mexican national bird."

When I come into the locker room that night, I see the Francisco twins and Wing and Sid all huddled around something they've got between them.

Naturally I think, there's something weird going on here. They probably are examining a shrunken testicles of an old pirate or looking into the eyeballs of a iguana. I want to see what it is.

It is only the sports page of today's paper that Sid is reading.

"We're one game out of first," Sid says when I come over. "They're singing our praises in Mexico City. They even got something about you, 'Henry Rogers, the flawless second baseman.'"

I was actually disappointed to find out they were just reading the paper, the way players in all locker rooms all over the world do, instead of casting some armadillo bones on the floor to tell us how we'll do tonight.

A moment later, there's panic in the locker room. The Franciscos are looking for the crates of magic balls. They've disappeared. Lots of whispering.

Sid reports, "They're convinced that the janitor was bought off by the players from the Guadalajara Giants, who are now in possession of a one-game lead and our balls."

He giggles at the way this comes out.

Sam Wing is weeping. His red silk bag is gone.

"And that's not all," Sid continues. "This time Guiterrez has more trouble on his hands than he bargained for."

Sid pauses for this to take full effect on me. I wait.

"He got the Cuban by giving Wally to the Slimy One. Now, all you have to do is look at Moon to see that he's finished too. He's practically a skeleton. I slid over to Moon yesterday. He was staring blankly into his locker at an old pin-up someone else pasted there. 'What's up, Moon?' I ask, 'looks like the world's got you down.'"

"'I guess, a bad case of Montezuma's Revenge,' he sighs. 'Can't put any weight on. I'm down twenty pounds from my best playing weight. And I'm not sleeping well. I dream all night of eyes staring at me.'"

12

Sid says, "Eyes? *Red eyes?*"

'Eyes,' is all he says. 'They could be red eyes.' Then he continues, 'I guess I toss in my sleep a lot too, because when I wake up sometimes, I see I've disturbed Henry's rest, cause he's walking around.'

"Then I get it," Sid says. "When Guiterrez gave Wally over to the One With the Pitchfork, part of the bargain that Guiterrez didn't know about was that the Dark Angel sent a vampire to get Moon. Henry Mungo's a blood-sucker sure. But now Guiterrez has to deal with the fact that he's got a Nosferatu on his hands. No wonder Mungo's hitting so good, he's getting a juicy transfusion every night. Moon's only got a few ounces of blood left in him, then he's a goner. Who will Henry and the Fanged Evil go for next? Guiterrez is the target. But he's slick – he's looking around for someone else to hand to the Keeper of the Furnace."

"Think what you're saying," I tell Sid. "Henry's a good player, that's all. Snap out of it."

"Did you even hear of Mungo before? If he's so good, how come you never heard of him before?"

"He's a Cuban player," I remind him, "I don't know anything about any Cuban players."

"Nosferatu," Sid says ominously. "Be sure you wear the cross I gave you. Pin it up by your neck. My bet is Guiterrez is the one who's next. Could be you though. The Master-of-the-Night is going to get someone soon."

"Quit the joking.'

"I'm going to put him to the test. Then you'll see. Henry Mungo, I mean."

"Test?"

"Tomorrow, bright and early, I'm heading down to the outdoor mercado and getting a big braid of garlic. I'm slipping it in his locker. I bet that's where he keeps his native earth. He won't be able to get to it. I already tried sprinkling some garlic salt on the bench in front of his locker. But he just sat down, and his ass didn't go on fire or turn to dust. I guess only the fresh stuff really works, don't you think? It'll be some sight when he opens his locker tomorrow night. The garlic gets him. He turns to jelly right before our eyes."

Sid does just what he says. Sid can't actually get Mungo's locker open, but before Henry gets in Sid hangs a bulb of garlic on the handle. Mungo walks up to it, removes the garlic, puts it to his nose to take in the fragrance, and cool as cucumber, says sweetly: "Why look here, someone made me a present of garlic. I love the stuff." And he breaks off a piece, rubs the skin off and pops it into his mouth.

"See," I whisper to Sid later. "You're wrong. That proves it."

"They're clever," Sid responds, "or else they wouldn't have lasted so long. They evolved. Only the vampires who could stand garlic survived. Now, the ones who are left relish garlic almost as much as blood. We just don't know what makes them recoil in horror now. It could be pizzas or rice pudding – anything."

I shake my head and give up.

But now we've lost three games in a row. Platon wails, "The Guadalajara Giants are cutting our balls into little pieces. We're finished."

Moon goes into the hospital in Mexico City. They'll finish him off there.

Monica comes out with the latest news from Betsy.

"The worst thing," she tells me, is that on the morning before Roger got those homers, they woke early and got it on. Twice. Not just twice. Rog did her from the rear both times, not perverted, you know, just doggie position. Betsy says she doesn't mind it from the back, but just once in a while, not twice a day for twenty-four days now. She doesn't even get to look at his face. 'But maybe it's just as well,' she says, 'because once I caught a glimpse of him behind me in the mirror, and he's not looking all that thrilled, he's gritting his teeth and looking desperate. Besides, before we get started every day, he's in the bathroom examining his tool and talking to it in a low voice, kind of pleading and giving it encouragement, saying things like, 'Come on old fella, do it for the gipper. Don't fail me now. We're pals ain't we?'"

"Betsy said to him, 'Okay, Rog, we can do it twice if we need to, but can't we do it in the good old-fashioned way?' He looks at me as if I'm his enemy. I think he hates me.'"

'You want to ruin my career, don't you? You don't care about me at all. You don't care about my streak. Have a heart and just turn over for a minute. I think I can get it in now.' He and his old pal are doing their best, but I don't think they'll be able to keep it up, so to speak, much longer.'"

"It's ridiculous," is all I say to Monica. But it's serious too. Rog can't last much longer.

But Monica must have gotten a little bit excited by all that sex talk, because she comes out and says pretty boldly: "Say, let's us try it. Maybe it'd be good?"

14

The love potion is working after all. I've got to get a look under the mattress to see if the doodles have disappeared.

We lose the fourth game in a row. The Voodoo boy's tongues are hanging out like beaten dogs. Now they have a cap from the Giants that they're sticking pins into. Sam Wing doesn't have any body hair to tear out, but he's lighting incense and leaving oranges in front of a little shrine he's made to the great god Buddoo. Guiterrez is looking peaked. Sid is probably right. Raphael is out of luck this time. His team is losing. Where do you go to manage when you are bust in the Mexican league? He'll be selling chiclets on a street corner in the Zona Rosa soon.

Henry's hitting better than ever, and Rog is doing ok too.

After we drop the fifth straight Rog is really down. The way he hangs around the locker room I can see he wants to talk. I'd rather not stay around because Monica's waiting for me in the room. Things have been going much better for us in the last few days.

Sid is almost the last to leave. As he goes he says, "The Flaming One is closing in. There's a big showdown coming." I see Sid has slipped a piece of pepperoni pizza under Mungo's locker.

Then Rog and I are alone.

"Two hits again tonight, old boy," I encourage him. ".381. Really incredible."

He's almost crying.

"I don't care about it anymore. Life is hell, isn't it?"

"You're doing great," I say.

"That Orioles guy isn't coming. I know it. He was never coming. It was just a rumor. It costs me too much to keep the streak going."

He's pausing, thinking it through, making a decision.

"Fuck it," he says. "Just fuck it. I'm giving it up. It's just not worth it. He's never coming. Fuck him if he does come. He can still see my average, can't he?"

"Right, he certainly can. But maybe he'll be there tomorrow night."

"No, I've decided, not one more day. This morning was it. I just can't take it anymore. Betsy will be glad anyway, even if I'm ruined. I'm glad too. I don't care. I can always work in the old man's commercial real estate company."

I reassure him that he is doing the right thing, but I don't let on I know the details. He goes out happy, saying, "I want to hurry back to tell Betsy. See you tomorrow. Thanks."

15

Let him go. He's forgotten that we drove out together in his car, and now I'll have to find a cab or take the bus.

Sid is waiting in the parking lot by his car.

"I saw Rog, I've been watching him. It's clear to me now. He looks a wreck, doesn't he? So does that broad of his. They're both fading away. Even all that power hitting of his is just the last fiery glow before the lights go out. It's not Guiterrez, but Rog and Betsy that the blood sucker is after. I don't know how he gets into their room at night. Vampires can climb walls, you know. I've seen it done in movies, like with suction cups. They have to be invited in, but all the stories make clear that women invite them. They are mesmerized by these fiends. Yeah, women are perverted that way, they go for the kind of gamy experiences, don'cha know? And Mungo is probably overjoyed to get some female blood after a long drink of Moon."

I'm reflecting that Sid hangs around bars where few women are present, which may explain something of his attitude. But he rushes on.

"Guiterrez has thrown the Cruncher-of-Sinners two bones this time, Rog and his squeeze. I think it'll buy the rest of us plenty of time."

He goes on in this same fashion all the way downtown and drops me off at my hotel. I'm anxious to see Monica. Maybe the love scribbles are working their way through my side of the mattress too.

The next night the Haitians and Sam Wing are passing the hat around.

"What's it for?" I ask Platon when he comes over to me.

"Okay, okay, Mister Henry," he says, "but don't let Mister Raphael hear a word of this. We found a guy who had a bat signed with marking pens by most of the Giants. It cost us six hundred dollars, but it's going to be well worth it. Broulee and Sam and I went out to a vacant lot with a five gallon can of gasoline and burned it. Now none of them will be able to hit worth a damn. They're fucked for good. You don't have to contribute. We shelled out for the team. But if you want, how about twenty-five or thirty bucks?"

I throw into the pot. All for one and one for all, I say. If setting a lousy bat on fire gives these guys confidence, well as good – they'll play better for it. If they believe they're sure winners they may actually become winners. It's common sense.

Rog comes in. He's still haggard, but all smiles.

"What a day," he sings, "What a great day. We had an early breakfast, lots of fruit for me, and Betsy had a Mexican brioche and tea.

16

We had a taxi driver take us to a big park where there's a great museum. I never thought much of it here but, you know, this town has its points."

Just to tease him and leave him wondering, I tell a fib: "Me, I had a big plate of huevos rancheros, beans and rice and real spicy salsa, with flour tortillas today."

"That makes me want to vomit," Rog says. "I'll never eat shit like eggs again, I'm telling you."

He thinks for a moment.

"I'm sad about the hitting streak, but I don't care. I've done good for weeks. If that don't impress the scouts, I'm through with them."

"Don't worry," I say, "Platon and Broulee have it all fixed up. They've sacrificed a bat, and they're convinced that the Giants can't hit us tonight. Lucky for Miguel, who's pitching. He needs all the help he can get. Maybe the scout will be here tonight."

Sam Wing has left messages for all the Giants in their boxes at the hotel, saying they've been incinerated, no hope remains for them. And it will work too. If the Giants have guys on their team who are as nuts as the ones on ours, they'll be scared shitless. There won't be a drop of live blood in them for even Henry to suck out.

Naturally, we win. But it's close. Henry strikes out three times in four at bats and hits a weak grounder off the end of his bat for an easy out. Rog does no better in the hit department. Henry's arms are hanging down like a puppet's on a hook. But Roger is happy. Betsy is at the ballpark, and even when Rog grounds out, she leaps to her feet and cheers him on.

I do ok, pretty much as usual. I get a solid hit in the first inning. Then in the ninth, leading off with the score zero-zero, I crack an outside pitch smooth as can be over the first baseman's head for a double. I steal third and come in on a flyout by Broulee, beating the throw by a mile. In the field I'm okay too, making a nice deep dive into the hole and a good throw to nip a runner. Nothing super spectacular. Mr. Reliable.

In the locker room Sid whispers to me, "Guiterrez has got his bead on the Nosferatu himself now. He's sending him back to the Fiery Furnace. It looks like Roger and Betsy will recover. You're in the clear too. Pretty soon Henry Mungo will be covered with his native earth for a long rest. He'll be rolling cigars in Hell."

Platon and Broulee and Wing are smiling, Rog and Betsy are happy as clams in high water, and Monica and I are doing fine. Even Sid has pretty much made his way back to reality.

17

I saunter into the hotel lobby.

As soon as I see him, I know who he is. He's sitting on a worn leather couch with an untouched greenish drink on the table in front of him, working on a cigar – probably Cuban.

He waves to me. I come over and he puts out his hand.

"I'm scouting for the Orioles. We've ever met? Jim McDougall."

"You used to play shortstop for the Braves ten-twelve seasons back."

"That's me."

"And with the Orioles now? That so?"

"I'm a Baltimore native. I love the place. What do you think of Baltimore?"

Small talk, but with an edge.

"Baltimore's great. The new stadium is great. The crab is great. Baltimore. It's got everything."

"Not you," he says.

"No, not me."

"You know what I'm saying. Tomorrow I'm going to send an email to the general manager and Casey –"

"I know Casey," I say. "He's managed the Orioles for ten years."

"He knows you. He likes you."

"I like him," I add, easy like.

"Yes, I'm going to say you'll be our second base man next year. Interested?"

"Sure."

"They'll do the details. I'm making a definite recommendation. Nice playing tonight. You and I will talk tomorrow. Lunch in this hotel?"

"Sure, lunch."

"I'll have a reply by then. It'll be the right reply, trust me."

"I do. Say, Roger is having a great winter."

"We've got outfielders up to there." He gives the chin gesture. "I came to take a peek at that Cuban, Mungo. But he can't hit a curveball worth a damn."

"I noticed that," I said. "But you don't get many good curveballs down here."

"Up there, he's a .230 hitter."

"All right, then," I say, "I'll see you right here at twelve."

"It's a deal."

18

He gestures toward two girls who are at the next table polishing off Zombies.

"Like one?" he asks. "We've sort of reached an understanding. I know you have a girl upstairs, but you could put her on ice for tonight. Sort of a special night for the Birds' new player. I'm kinda partial to the one with her hair put up, but if you like her, take her. We could make a night of it. Want to try your luck?"

Luck. It's a tempting offer, but I don't need that kind of luck. I shake my head. I say, "The girl who's upstairs – she's enough luck for me."

"You wouldn't want to leave me with two broads on my hands," he says smiling, joking. "Two's a bit over my limit."

"Say, they've got some pretty good love potions down here," I tell him.

But I know the sort of life he leads, traveling and scouting and having to party. It's exhausting. He'll give the girls a pleasant tip and a wink and happily hit the sack.

"One's my limit," I say. I'm thinking of Monica and of the magic starting with us. I'll just ask her right off, "What kind of place should we get in Baltimore, huh?"

THE BOY WHO BECAME A BLOOMER GIRL

When I was a girl, Smoky Joe Hood said, I learned a lot about playing baseball.

That was it, the way his best stories always started, without a warmup, with some amazing assertion. When that happened, no one interrupted. Joe told stories the way he once pitched complete games.

My father was born on a farm in Kanapolis, Kansas. Smokey Joe continued, That's in the Smoky Hills, in case you don't know it. Some writers in the newspapers claimed that it's from the Smoky Hills that I got my nickname, but the truth is, that name was coined my first season when some damn fool sportswriter was trying to give an impression of my fastball.

Anyway, Dad always said that even when he was little on his Dad's farm he knew he didn't want to be a farmer. It was tough in Kansas in the eighties— droughts, insects, foreclosures. Some farmers committed suicide. Others returned East with signs on their wagons saying: "In God we trusted. In Kansas we busted." Dad went to college in Hays and became an attorney.

I would have wanted only to become an attorney too, I guess, except that on Memorial Day in 1908, when I was ten years old, Dad took the whole family to a baseball game. It was one of those barnstorming teams who came to Hays to challenge the locals. The name of the team was the "Veterans." I sort of remember that some players had been in the Spanish-American War with Teddy Roosevelt's Rough Riders.

They certainly walloped the Hays Elks Club team, 16-2. I rooted for both sides. It was the game that got me. From the first crack of the bat I was a goner. A man near us was recording the game on a scorecard. I begged my father to teach me how to do that, but he didn't know how. It was the first time I discovered there was something my father didn't know, and I understood then that to learn all I needed to know I would have to go to others.

From then on, I wanted to be a baseball player, nothing else. I knew Dad wouldn't go along. We were "drys" and regular church-goers. We didn't go in much for fun, even for hugs and kisses and stuff like that. But we were big on "being responsible" and "living up to your promise." That meant being an attorney.

He was respected. He was elected to the Kansas legislature in our district and when he returned to his private practice four years later everyone said he had represented his constituents with honor.

My Dad would tell his dream pretty often: "It would be dandy for me if I could put out a shingle that read 'Hood and Hood/Attorneys-at-Law."

I got away with playing ball only because it was for kids.

By the time I was twelve, I was a pretty fair pitcher and hitter, maybe the best in both departments among the boys I played with Saturday mornings, even though I hadn't had my growth spurt year and I was still as slim as a willow, "a beautiful boy," my Aunt Laura always said. To see me now you wouldn't think it, I know, so don't make any wisecracks about my faded beauty.

Every now and then a team would barnstorm through our area, but I could only catch the games played on Saturdays. No Sunday baseball for us.

I wanted to be a pitcher, of course. By 1910 or '11 Walter "Big Train" Johnson was my hero. He was even born in Kansas, in Humboldt. I practiced hurling every day. On an abandoned barn wall I painted a rectangular strike zone. Then I stepped off sixty feet and used a broken off piece of a plank to make a pitching "rubber." In the beginning I threw stones at the siding. My mom had saved rubber bands forever and I borrowed a bunch of them and made a ball covered with adhesive tape.

One Saturday during a boys game over by the town of Catherine, under a tree near the edge of the field a man stood quietly watching the game. In my mind I made up a story that he was a big league scout and that he would sign me up to pitch for the Washington Senators.

I was wrong – but not entirely. After the game ended, he caught up with me.

"Good game, kid," he said. "You got the stuff."

"Thanks, mister. But I've pitched better lots of times."

"Sure you have. How would you like to play a couple of games tomorrow for my team?"

I wanted to say yes right away and to begin my destiny right there, but tomorrow would be Sunday. "Never on Sunday" meant baseball in Kansas.

"Well, I mean, maybe. What's your team?" I was hedging, but I knew I'd have to say no.

"Well, it's like this," he says. "We're a barnstorming team and we've challenged two of the local teams to matches. It's a double-

21

header, one game against a team called the 'River Runners,' and the other against the 'Pioneers' club."

I had seen both play. The first team was composed of a brawling bunch of roustabouts who worked along the Smoky Hill river, and the other was a union team. Those were teams of grownup men.

"So, do you want to play?" he asked.

It made me a little afraid. If he had really been a scout for the Senators, I would surely have said, "Sign me up." But to pitch against the "River Runners" was scary. And on Sunday.

"I dunno. Maybe I should give my pitching arm a rest tomorrow."

"What's the matter? You'll do ok. Won't your mother let you play on Sunday?"

That was a challenge. No thirteen year old boy could walk away from something like that, even if it was a duel with Aaron Burr or a sword fight with Blackbeard. Even if he had to lie to play on Sunday.

"Sure, I'll play," I said. But I felt I had put my head in a noose.

"Good. Look, the trouble is, we are short a player. We only have eight. One of the regulars is sick. We need somebody or else we'd forfeit the games. It's winner-take-all, and we need to be the winners."

"I'll do my best," I replied, summoning up my deepest voice, but to tell the truth my voice hadn't changed yet and it was still high-pitched.

"You don't have to do anything," he said. "The rest of the team will do that. They're a great bunch. You'll see. You just have to show up so's we have nine players on the field. And don't worry about your pitching arm. We have a doozy of a hurler. You can plant yourself in right field."

Maybe for my first big games against the Pioneers and the River Runners, right field would be a good place to be.

"Ok," I said, "I'll play right."

The man led me to the tree where he had stood to watch the game. He picked up a package he had left there.

"See, my name is Billy, Billy Bunny. I'm the business manager, coach, and all-around arranger of everything. What I got in this package is a uniform for you. I want you to show up at the Fairgrounds tomorrow at one o'clock wearing it. Maybe you better unwrap it now. I picked you out because of your size. The uniform will fit you. It's almost brand new."

That really hurt my feelings. I couldn't believe that what he said was true. My *size*! Didn't he notice my skill? Couldn't he see that on the diamond I was head and shoulders above all the other guys my age?

22

I'll show him tomorrow, I vowed. I'll perform some spectacular feat. But I didn't say anything. I opened the package. Out came a red cap with "BG" in blue letters on it.

"Try it on," he demanded.

I did.

"Fits fine," he said.

"It's a little loose," I said.

"Don't worry, it's perfect – it won't be loose."

He picked up another piece of uniform.

"Hold the blouse up to you," he asked.

I did. It was bright red.

"It'll fit fine. I knew it," he said.

I turned the shirt around the read the name of the team.

Then I had the surprise of my life.

In bold blue letters the shirt said: BLOOMER GIRLS.

I was dumbstruck. I couldn't think of anything to say. Before I could even begin to gather my wits, Billy was saying: "Swell. Hold the skirt up. Let's see."

He frowned.

"The waist's a little loose. Hold onto this safety pin in case you need it. We wouldn't want the skirt to slip down below your bloomers when you're chasing a fly would we?"

He laughed.

It was no laughing matter.

Two other items remained. One was a pair of bloomers to wear under the short skirt. The other was a curly blonde wig. I picked these up and stared at them in amazement.

"It's made of real human hair. Don't lose it. Cost me a pretty penny. Never used till now," Billy said. It'll look great on you. Not a soul in the world would be able to tell it from a real head of hair."

"But this is a girl's team," I said.

"I told you that in the first place, didn't I?" Billy answered. "Yeah, the Bloomer Girls. Heard of us? It's the best little gimmick in the world. Took me months to put the team together. We challenge all the tough-guy teams. Both teams put up pots, winner gets them. We've got a peach of a team. Every girl is a star. Never lose. At first the men's teams refuse to play us when they hear that it's girls who are challenging them. 'A girl's team, pssst!' they spit. 'We don't play girls. Girls should stay in the kitchen. What kind of baseball can girls play? It wouldn't be fair.'"

23

Bunny continued 'Oh, I guess you've heard of us. You're afraid we'll beat you. I guess you heard that we slaughtered the 'Cattlemen' team in Abilene. I guess you don't want to risk the embarrassment of losing to the Bloomer Girls.' I'd pause to let the steam build up a little in them, and then I'd add, 'Well, I could ask the girls if they'd be willing to spot your team a few runs, just to give you a fighting chance.' That would do it.

'We'll spot *you* a few runs more like it, and then knock your bloomers off,' they'd say.

That'd give me a chance to joke, 'They'll be no bloomers coming off that day, boys. This is a clean team. Just a clean game of baseball.'

"The River Runners is a swell team," I tell Billy. "Girls couldn't beat them."

"Wait and see. You'll be on the winning team, I bet you."

"I don't bet," I told him. "My Dad is really strict about gambling."

"Just a figure of speech," Billy smiled. "But mine's a safe bet anyway."

I looked at the uniform dubiously.

"That's Sally's uniform. You're just her size. She was great in the field."

"So where is she – Sally?"

"Well, sort of indisposed right now. Put on too much weight around the middle. I guess the bloomers came off Sally once too often. I guess she really did play the field."

I'm sure I turned red in the face at this kind of risqué talk.

"I don't even know your name," Billy said.

"It's Joe."

"Good. Jo it is then. Let's make it Jo Alcott for the lineup. You'll be a little woman for a day."

I said nothing.

"Ok, kid," Billy said. "You know when and where. Be sure you arrive all suited up. We got to have our nine players. And," he paused for emphasis, "and don't forget to wear that wig."

He paused again. "It'll look real cute on you," he said.

I had to think up some excuse to miss Sunday dinner for the first time in my life. Helping my friend Charlie with his homework would be considered a good deed. With his Dad sick, and all the chores falling on him, he probably could have used a little help with school. I used that story on my mother. She sort of hesitated, ready to say no.

"What's the homework?" my father called from the next room where he was leafing through a history of Rome.

I told a whopper. "It's History," I said. "We're reading about the Code of Hammurabi. We have to write a big paper comparing it to the laws in the Old Testament, Leviticus, Kings, and First Samuel."

When I came out with that lie, instinctively, naturally, with not an ounce of calculation or premeditation, then in one white-hot searing flash I saw my destiny before me. I would lie and cheat and break my parents' hearts and become a baseball player. And do it all without remorse or even regret.

"Oh, Lillian, let the boy miss dinner this time. He can have some nice leftovers when he gets back," my father called.

At that my Mom raised her hands to her temples, then dropped them limply to her sides.

"All right," she conceded. "But be back before dark."

Just before I arrived at the Fairgrounds, I found a nice clump of bushes and changed into the uniform. I pulled the wig down on my head and clamped by BG cap on it.

Now I became a girl, a Bloomer Girl.

It made all the difference. I found myself walking different, like a girl, the way I saw girls walk. I started to hold my hands the way they did, and not swing my shoulders and tramp like a boy. I didn't want it or help it, that's just the way it happened, and that's all I can tell you about it even now, after all these years.

When I was still about a hundred feet away from the visitor's bench on the third base side, where I saw my teammates assembling, Billy started toward me and led me back to the spot where the girls all turned toward me.

"This is Jo," he said, "I found her over by the town of Catherine yesterday. She's going to take Sally's place for this game, then we'll replace Sally permanently. Jo, this is" – and here he named in turn, "Alice, Rowena, Patsy, Emmerline, Lucy, Lena, Carrie, and Colleen."

That was the whole team. Add Jo to them and we've got the Bloomer Girls nine.

I was the smallest and slimmest of all the girls. Alice towered over me. She gave my hand a powerful shake. Emmy gave me a little hug.

25

The other girls smiled and made dove sounds. It felt good to be a part of a team, a real team that barnstormed for money. I couldn't say it exactly this way then, but now with all the years that have flowed between, I can say that in the joyful moment of greeting and comradeship I felt that I was just one of the girls.

"Jo's playing right field," Bunny explained, "where there's little action. That means, Rowena, you take Sally's position at third....Ok, let's get ready to beat these gorillas."

From where we stood, looking over the diamond toward the home team's bench on the first base side, they seemed like gorillas too – big blubbery beefy guys who looked sweaty and smelling. They gave the impression that their breaths reeked of something horrid, like limburger cheese or gin. They were laughing and gesticulating in a vulgar fashion.

"I know, I know," Lena said from beside me. "When I was a beginning Bloomer Girl I thought, 'Why do we have to play *them*?' Guys would be all right if only they were more like girls. But you'll get used to it. The time before the game is the hardest part. They think they're such big bugs. But you'll see – you'll feel different when the game is over and they slink off quietlike."

She put her hand on my shoulder in quiet commiseration. She was a sweet girl, Lena. The last time I heard anything of her she had six grandchildren.

Anyway, we practiced for fifteen minutes on the field. We outfielders – Lucy and Colleen and I – tossed a ball to each other and practiced long throws as if we were trying to nail a runner at home. Billy hit some high fungos out to us. All of us rotated to the plate to bat.

I began to feel better about being able to measure up on the team, for to tell the truth, the girls were pitiable players. It was a scandal. Wherever they came from, the standards must have been really low if it were true that they ever won a single game. Some of the easy flies that Bunny hit to them Colleen and Lucy muffed or misjudged. When I threw a liner to Colleen as if to a catcher, she let the ball skip right over her shoulder. At bat they were no better. Alice pitched nice fat balloons to them so slow that she could almost have walked the ball to the plate and handed it to the batters. And still they swung futilely, popped up, or bounced easy grounders around the infield. Me, I snagged every ball hit to me. And at bat, I hit a few hard ones that might have gone for hits. When I finished my swings, I heard one of the loudmouthed bruisers say, "Well, lookie, that little muffin playing right field is the star of the team. Who would have thunk it?"

26

I turned red with anger, I guess it was, or shame, because I had come to the same conclusion myself. It was going to be a long, dismal afternoon.

But when Billy came back, he was elated. "I got them to double the doubled pot," he said. The girls laughed into their gloves and looked at each other sideways.

I wanted to save my new pals and say, "Take a look at those big galoots. They can throw, they can hit, they can catch." The River Runners were loud in their appreciation of each other as they practiced: " Swell hit, Bill." "Nice catch, George, over the head running away." "Great peg into home." "That'll knock their bloomers off!"

The thing was, I felt a lot of admiration for these big strong guys. They weren't serious men like my Dad, of course. They were goodtimers, and they had the kind of rollicking team I wanted to be on.

But I didn't say anything. I decided that I'd stick by my team. If they went down, I'd go down with them. Nine musketeers. They had taken me in without reservation and I vowed to do the same for them.

Alice must have seen me looking a little blue, because she came over to me and said, "Don't worry, Jo, we'll be all right." She was the tallest girl on the team, nearly six feet and I let her give me the boost I needed.

It only lasted a moment.

As the visitors, we came up first, and all my fears were realized.

"You're first up," Billy said – to *me*. "Look here, let's play a little strategy on them. Do you know what a bunt is? Yes? Try a bunt. They won't expect it."

"Sure, I know what a bunt is."

"Go to it."

The first pitch came in high. I knew enough to look for a low one, but just to fool them I made a vicious swing at it, intending to miss. Poor as it was, I was using a little strategy of my own. I did miss – by a mile. But I saw the third baseman move back two steps.

The next pitch was low enough, and I laid a roller along the third base line, too far for the catcher to chase it. He ran to back up first. The third baseman charged. I scooted as fast as I could as soon as the ball left the bat, and I crossed the bag before the throw.

I thought with satisfaction, no matter what else happens now, I got us a hit. They can't no hit us. I felt that somehow I had maintained the pride of the team. Besides, the girls were cheering me. That felt swell.

Billy was coaching at first now. "Take a little lead," he whispered. "And when you hear the crack of a bat, don't look, just run. Alice is coaching third. Watch her when you round second." Billy made occult hand signals toward Patsy at the plate.

I took a lead. The guy playing first base guarded the bag. "Watch out girlie," he snarled, "we'll pick you off sure."

I stared at second base as if I could make it come closer. Then the crack came. I ran. The ball bounced about three feet in front of me on its way to right field. I hit the base and saw Alice giving me a big come on and so I came. She was standing right in back of third base so I could see her and the bag at the same time. When she put her arms out to the side with her palms down I figured that meant slide, and I went into a hook slide with my skirts flying and my bloomers ballooning. I was already holding onto the base with my right hand when the throw arrived, but the baseman jabbed a hard tag into my hip anyway. "Hey, watch it," I shouted, leaping to my feet with balled fists. Good thing Alice slipped between me and the chump playing third – he outweighed me by at least hundred pounds.

"Calm down, Jo," she said. "You made a great hook. Where'd you learn that?"

For the third baseman to hear she said, "Gosh, wasn't that lucky? Patsy made a perfect hit-and-run by accident."

Carrie swung at the first two pitches, both outside the strike zone, and missed them. It began to look to me as if their pitcher was just tossing the ball in, with no plan, no control. On the third pitch she connected and lofted a fly to left. The fielder backed up a dozen steps.

"You know to tag-up when he gloves it, right?" Alice called. "Get ready, I'll tell you when.

When!"

I sped toward home. Billy, who was coaching behind the home plate, stood with his palms up and I crossed the plate standing. But Patsy got a late start, I guess, trying for third, because on the relay they threw her out by a mile. I turned to see her slide, though she was a dead duck. Then I heard the third baseman cry "Ouch." Seems she accidentally nipped him with her spikes. He hopped around on one foot for a minute, glaring at Patsy's back as she walked toward our bench. And then he said gruffly and loud, "It's nothing. Just a scratch. Get on with it."

I got a big greeting when I got back to the bench. "You broke the ice, Jo." "You got us a run." "You made that hit-and-run go!" "Pretty

28

fleet on your feet, girl." Patsy said in a low voice, "That third baseman will think twice before giving another girl a bullshit tag, the way he jabbed you, Jo." She gave me a whack on the back.

Alice, batting cleanup, didn't get a good swing and tapped an easy grounder to the pitcher.

Meanwhile, Billy had been over on the other side of the field talking to their manager, a thin-faced, tweaked-nosed scalper with little beady eyes like a magpie. I suppose they were discussing something about the lineup.

Billy threw her glove to Alice and said, low, "Sure, I doubled the pot easy." Alice walked out to the mound, tossed a few to Carrie, then said lazily to the ump, "I'm ready."

Then the blinders fell from my eyes. No more slow pitches. The first pitch she threw came in as fast as a musket shot. To the batter the sphere must have looked the size of a minnie ball. Alice gave pitching lessons – inside, outside, fast ball, curve ball, fork ball, drop, fast ball again, slow curve, knuckle ball with a slippery elm spitball here and there. For three innings she went through the lineup without a man laying a bat on even one of her deliveries. In the fourth she took off some smoke and the lead off whammed a liner right over third base, a sure double, but Rowena laid out flat in the air and trapped it in her outstretched glove. It was a piece of pure acrobatics, as good a catch as any third baseman ever made.

"Let me give you an easy one," Alice told the next batter. She sent the ball in at, say, sixty m.p.h., about half of the speed she could throw, and he did hit the ball deep into center. Colleen trotted toward the fence casually, turned around and caught the ball one-handed behind her back.

That was the game. It was only beginning, but the River Runners looked like River-Rats, they were so beaten.

When we came up at the end of the fourth, Alice said with a cheery grin, "Ok, before the Pioneers arrive, let's have a little fun. The girls batted through the lineup. Colleen hit from both sides. The River Runners' pitcher was so rattled that I was able to wait him out for a walk. Their outfielders got good exercise that afternoon. Alice gave them a rest by knocking the ball into a stand of trees twenty yards beyond the fence. They didn't have to chase that one.

At the end of the fourth inning we were in the lead 14-0.

At the end of the sixth inning, their little weasel manager came over to Billy and handed him the quadruple pot. He was sour and he showed it. "We don't want to play with girls no more. Should never have

29

agreed to do it in the first place, it's not natural. We'll give you the game," he said in a condescending way, but we all knew that the River Runners didn't want to be around, shamefaced, when the Pioneers players started to trickle in. They walked away from the field talking loud and swaggering, trying not to look beaten. I knew what Carrie meant when I heard her say to Lucy: "It's their wives I feel sorry for. They'll be in for a hard time tonight. Might be some bruises before morning."

She's right, I thought, men can be awful mean, and I felt proud in a strange way to be one of the Bloomer Girls, who would go to bed happily that night without giving or taking any abuse.

We didn't have to put on a show of incompetence for a second game. When the Pioneers arrived, shoving and jostling each other gaily, Billy just told their manager: "Well, the girls are all tuckered out from playing that earlier game. They don't want any warm-ups, or else they might get exhausted – women, you know, maybe some of them are having their monthly time, I suppose – so you just do your practicing and then we'll start....But say, how's about doubling the pot, just for the fun of it?"

The Pioneer manager, a rubbery, roly-poly Santa Claus, asked, "How'd you do against the River Runners?"

Billy put on his saddest puss, looked down at the ground and mumbled feebly, "Well, we've done a lot better other times."

"Well, just for the fun of it," Fatty Arbuckle agreed, "let's double."

I was sitting at the end of the bench. Lena was next to me.

"Alice is great," I said to her. "She's the best player I ever saw. You're all the best players."

"But Alice is the best," Lena agreed. "You don't know who she is, do you? Alice Johnson."

It didn't ring any bells with me.

"Alice Johnson. Walter Johnson's big sister. She's the one taught him to pitch. But she's faster than he is. He says so himself. Walter "Big Train" Johnson. She's the locomotive of the big train. She should be in the majors. If the Senators had the two of them, maybe they'd win a pennant sometime. But to the Big Leagues, she's just a girl."

Alice, Big Train, and me, I thought. Maybe something will rub off on me the way it did on Walter.

Actually, that's the way it worked out. But I'm not to that part of my story yet.

Alice didn't toy with the Pioneers. Judging from their batting practice and the quality of their pitcher, they were a better team than the River Runners, who had consumed a lot of beer on the sly. But we hit right from the beginning – that is, the other girls did. And Alice simply threw the ball past them, strike after strike. After two innings the score was 12-0. Billy visited the puffy manager to suggest that darkness might be approaching – though the sun, in fact, was at its pinnacle for the day – and that the game could be called with us ahead, and no disgrace.

The Pioneers shouted Billy down. "We've got an unblemished record and we're not going to lose to a bunch of skirts and bloomers," one said. Another added, "That gosh dern pitcher is about burned out. She can't last another inning. We'll whup her after all."

Billy shrugged his shoulders. "No offense meant," he said apologetically.

"None taken," the other manager said.

But Alice fanned the next six Pioneers in the same methodical way, and they were really angry.

As I began to trot in from right field, the Pioneer right fielder came toward me to take his position. He carried his glove in front of him. But when he got about ten feet from me he let his glove slip to the ground.

I sure must have turned all colors of scarlet at that. There in plain sight was his thing sticking out of his fly.

I looked at his face. There was no mistake. He was grinning in a sick way.

"That's what you really want, cutie," he whispered. "How'd you like to catch that in your little glove?"

Over this pervert's shoulder I could see Alice near the pitcher's mound aim a roundhouse at the opposing pitcher, while the other girls were staring at the sights they were seeing. The whole team of Pioneers was doing the snake-charmer act. Even their manager had his weenie out, I guess, but his belly was so big or his penis was so tiny he couldn't get it in sight. It was pathetic and funny at the same time.

The Pioneer pitcher crumpled.

Alice looked my way. Maybe this sort of thing had happened to the Bloomer Girls before or maybe she knew that the others could take care of themselves. But she had pity on me, and I saw her running toward right field.

"Hey, honey," the Pioneer right fielder said, "don't look over there. Here's a big chaw of sweet tobacco for you. Take a gander at it."

31

Actually I did, and now he had an erection. I was astonished. He was getting excited over *me*. But what I felt most was how low a thing it was for him to do. So is that what guys want girls to feel – humiliated and dirty? – because that's what I felt. But I also felt how mean a guy can be to use such a dirty trick as a way of winning when he's a loser otherwise.

By this time I could see that Alice had nearly gotten to us. She was about twenty feet away when she set her feet and called out "Hey!"

She still gripped the ball that she had been carrying to the mound. When he turned toward her she let it fly and it hit him somewhere below the belt. I couldn't see exactly where it landed down there, because now his back was turned to me. But he said "Ooof," went down on his face and made no further sound.

Alice stepped over his body and came to me.

"I suppose he's dead," she said indifferently. "How are you?"

"I'm ok," I answered, but I was surprised to hear my voice crack.

We walked back to the bench where the other girls surrounded us. "I told to mine," Lucy said, "Is that all? Fish it all out, let's have a look at it!" Lena interjected, "I fell on the ground laughing." "I," Colleen added, "I said, 'I do believe there's a bicycle pump around somewhere. You've got a flat tire, mister.'" Patsy was next: "I said, 'Wow, this is great. I was going to go fishing tomorrow. I could sure use that inchworm there.'" Rowena jumped in: "I looked at him quizzically and asked, 'Is there something I'm supposed to see? Poor fellow, you must have had a serious injury on the farm.'" Each girl added her appreciation of the event, while, behind us, the Pioneers were dragging the pitcher and right fielder from the diamond. Billy was over by first base talking seriously to the manager, who had buttoned his fly.

Alice sat me down on the bench. I felt woozy and weak. I was trying to join in the uproarious good humor of the Bloomer Girls, but failing pretty miserably.

"You'll be fine," Alice said. The team gathered around me. "It's a shame to pull this nasty trick on you, after all you've been through. Don't think that we haven't noticed your secret."

So they knew all along that I was a boy, I thought. Of course, how could they not? Probably they think I'm just like those other fellars.

"You know?"

"Jo, any woman can see that you're wearing a wig. Lena noticed it as soon as you walked over."

She paused with a look of sympathy. The smiles on the faces of all the other girls faded too.

"You must have had a terrible disease for you to have lost all your hair. And to be feeling ashamed of being bald and all, and then to have those goofs flash you like that."

Lena said, "We just wanted you to know that we think you're really brave to join our team today."

"You're going to be a great woman someday," Rowena said.

"You're a real woman, now," Emmy said, "though just a wee bit of one." They all giggled at that and I giggled a little too.

The most outlandish thought entered my mind then. Maybe since the time I put on the Bloomer Girls uniform I really had become a girl. Maybe it was like one of those magical garments in the fairy tales, the kind of cloak that makes you invisible or superhuman, and this one had really made me a girl. The thought took hold of me so much that I itched to check it out. But, surrounded by my team, I was too embarrassed to feel down there. And later on I forgot about it until I was back in my strange boy clothes again. So now I'll never know.

Billy strode in. "Victory!" he said. "Of course they forfeited the game, but with our agreement that we'd speak no more about this game and its concluding – shall I say? – errors, they doubled the already double purse. Now, let's get out of here before somebody thinks of tar and feathers. 'Bloody Kansas,' you know. We're heading toward Nebraska next. Fresh pickings."

"Guess you won't be coming with us," Carrie said to me. "It was swell having you on our side. You're a sport, Jo."

Billy gave out a piece of information. "I sent a telegram two days ago to Jennie Manush – you remember she used to play short? – to join us in Beloit before we go on to Hastings."

Some of the girls said "So long" and I got a few pats on the butt, and then I was alone.

It took me a while to feel like a boy again.

I thought and thought about all sorts of things as I trudged home. I didn't like it that I lied to my parents. I didn't want to break their hearts. Sure, maybe I'd try to be a baseball player, but why couldn't I be an attorney too and have a sweet wife to cherish all my days? If I could be good enough to be a Bloomer Girl, maybe I could be a man too, and not go to hell.

So right off I told them what I had done. To my astonishment Mom said, "I'm proud of you for telling the truth," and she popped right out of her chair and gave me a real bear hug, the first one I had gotten from her since I don't know when.

Dad sort of glowered at me. I guess he was sort of picturing the shingle of "Hood and Hood/Attorneys at Law" falling down.

I said, "I want to be a baseball player, Dad, like you wanted to be a lawyer, not a farmer like your dad, but I want to be a lawyer too. Maybe someday we'll be putting up a sign saying "Hood and Hood."

He brightened at that. And Mom brought me a plate of cold chicken from Sunday dinner. I sure was starving.

I wrote to the Bloomer Girls in Beloit and told them about the trick Billy and I had played and how bad I felt at fooling them.

I expected that they'd treat me like an unwanted dog, but they didn't. Lena wrote back, "Joe, you're the best girl any boy has ever been. You were really one of the Bloomer Girls for that day."

I told them that I was going to be a baseball player and an attorney, and Lucy wrote back, "Then start by making a law giving us girls the vote, and then make them take us into the big leagues."

"I'll do my best," I promised. And I did. I marched with the suffragettes too. I even carried a sign once that someone thrust in my hand, reading: A MAN CAN VOTE. WHY CAN'T I?

Alice sent a letter of invitation: "Come around next year when we're in Kansas, when you're bigger and stronger and filled out and we'll work on it."

And she did teach me until I went to Yale with a baseball scholarship, and then to the Red Sox, and got my law degree at Harvard.

I guess you know about the game I pitched against Big Train. I was a rookie and was on a winning streak. And he had won ten straight.

He beat me one to nothing. But I didn't care. After the last out, Walter came over to me. He was a real gentleman. "I've only seen one other person beside myself pitch in just the way you do," he said.

"I know," I said, "We both pitch just like a girl."

OUR LADY'S FIELDER

Father Philip Gardiner pretends to be relaxed.

He says to his assistant pastor, "Mrs. Brevold hasn't made a fuss about Father Fred for a whole week now."

"May it remain so," Father Lou responded with almost papal solemnity. He considered crossing himself to give full expression to his pious wish, but he thought better of it and merely smiled wanly, as he believed a martyr would do.

The very next morning Mrs. Lucinda Brevold made her third appearance in the rectory, spoiling Father Gardiner's lunch.

The first time she visited him with her complaint he had adopted the pastoral attitude of benign compassion. He petted and soothed her – at least he attempted to do so. He barely listened to her allegations. Father Fred, Father Fred, he chanted in his mind, as if chastising a misbehaving child.

"It's merely a game," he insisted. "By the way, did you know that Father Fred was once a famous baseball player? Maybe he'll even be a Hall-of-Famer someday. That seems to explain things, doesn't it?"

He hoped that would settle matters, but he was disappointed.

Upon hearing her second complaint, he tried a different approach.

"Dear Mrs. Brevold – perhaps I might call you Lucinda?" – she glared at him – "Mrs. Brevold, let me counsel with Father Williamson. Doubtless he's unaware of the impression his activities might convey."

"See that you do," she said, then stomped out of the rectory, shaking the hand blown diamond-leaded window panes. Her ferocity surprised Father Philip. From life with his mother he had acquired an unexamined opinion that wealthy women are irrational. So when he next saw Fred, he still treated the matter carelessly. He merely said, "Father, you know that we priests must remember that some of our activities might make a bad impression upon the laity." Fred looked at him with no sign of comprehension, and with a paternal pat on Fred's shoulder Philip let the matter drop.

"A word to the wise," he said to himself. But he didn't pause to consider whether or not Fred Williamson was one of the wise.

Mrs. Brevold was not to be taken lightly. She was a handsome woman, stately as a great mansion, dignified as a Roman statue. At her prime she would have been stunning, and she was still grand. The property on which the church, the rectory, the school buildings, the two golf courses, and the luxurious new estates all stood, had been in her

35

family for generations. At one time, the land had been occupied by Indians, from whom the patriarch Brevold had secured it in a hurried and rather extralegal way. Just before he died, Lucinda's father sold the whole great tract to a consortium of venture capitalists, developers, bankers, and contractors. This left the fortune squeezed by Brevold generations out of the earth and the Indians in the vault of the Farmers and Merchants' Bank and made Lucinda the wealthiest woman in the state.

On her third visit, she began; "Father Gardiner, on my first visit you told me that Father Williamson was once a famous baseball player. You asserted that this fact 'explained everything.' I gave serious consideration to your proposition. But I concluded that it explained nothing whatsoever, nothing, nothing at all." In her eyes the glint of a banked fire flashed.

"Of course, you're right. But give Father Williamson the benefit of his simplicity. Between those of us who know, isn't there something endearing, even something admirable, in his naiveté?"

She gave the same answer: "Nothing, nothing whatsoever. I find nothing admirable about him, Father. I respect his position as an ordained man of God. I venerate the calling that he follows, and I appreciate the good works that I presume he performs. But I hold a low opinion of him personally."

"Of his character?" Father Philip wondered.

"Of his sanity," she said, adding with some menace: "And I expect more of you."

"I'll handle it," Father Phillip said with all the reassurance he could muster. Then he tried once more to win her favor. Her villa on the actual Ligurian coast was famous. She had lived in Italy for twenty years and he had studied Italian at Yale for four.

"*Chen e pensa?*" he asked, expecting her to reply politely that she liked the idea of handing it over to him.

But she snapped sternly: "*Non me piace tanto.*" Lucinda could be ungraciously imperious in seven languages.

Next, she performed her legendary exit *con furioso*, rattling the diamond panes even more than on the two previous occasions.

Father Gardiner went to lunch soon after, but his stomach felt queasy and he picked at his lobster. Both of his curates joined him.

36

Father Fred was quiet. Ten years after his last baseball game he still had the same spare, lanky look. When he was not in motion he looked awkward, uncoordinated, but when swinging a bat or snagging flies he resembled a runaway train.

Now he sat loose and disjointed, looking uncomfortable, having finished a turkey sandwich. Six Maui chips remained decoratively on his plate. A half-full glass of O'Doul's non-alcoholic beer remained.

"Well, I'll be going," Fred mumbled.

The two other priests made no objection, knowing that each day after lunch Fred would walk over to the church and sit for an hour in the left side chapel before the statue of the Virgin. They supposed he prayed. No one asked.

He left.

"Lucinda Brevold?" Father Lou asked.

"Of course."

"I knew it as soon as I saw your look."

"No one else can get to me the way she can."

"I know."

Father Lou had a Ph. D. in clinical psychology. His voice became therapeutic.

"What is it *this* time?"

"What else?"

"And she says – what?" Lou inquired.

The pastor had not confided in anyone about Lucinda's accusations. They were too strange, too ludicrous, too outlandish. To take them seriously would be to brand either Lucinda or Fred insane. In Phil's book, it was unthinkable that anyone with hundreds of millions could be truly insane, and Fred was too ordinary to be bizarre. So he had been in a quandary. But now he needed Father Lou's assistance. He had to take him into his confidence.

"She says that Fred is demented."

"Fred? Rather unlikely, don't you think?"

"Anyone would agree with you. But –"

"But?"

"She has facts, or she says she has facts."

"Nothing about little girls or boys, I hope," Lou said warily.

"Not *that*, thank God." Phil breathed his first sigh of relief in an hour. "No, nothing like that."

"There's no probability of criminal charges, or a suit then?"

"Not in the slightest. Thank God, again."

"If you don't mind," Lou said, with some return of his therapist's tone, "why don't you tell me *what* it is? Or did she swear you to confidence?"

"Far from it," Phil said, animatedly now. "So far as she is concerned, she would be ready to go on national television to denounce him."

"For? –"

"I hate to say it. Sacrilege. She wants him removed from the priesthood. Excommunicated, if possible. Stripped of his faculties. Prevented from saying mass. Confined to a sanitarium. Kept under close watch."

"That's a mouthful," Lou responded. "But what's he *done*?"

"She says…she *says* that he drives out to a remote meadow, lays down a home plate, sets up a portable pitching machine, fills it with balls, and…."

Father Lou waited now for almost a minute.

"And," Phil finally completed the sentence, "he hits baseballs to the Virgin Mary!"

"Baseballs. The Virgin Mary," Father Lou repeated blankly.

"Not the Virgin Mary *herself*, or course. Mrs. Brevold says that he brings a statue of the Virgin Mary that he has taken from the chapel in St. Augustine's, and sets her up in center field. And hits balls to her."

"Hits balls to her?"

"Yes, balls."

"Well," Father Lou let down his guard completely, "that's disgusting."

"I've hardly wanted to believe it myself," Philip lamented, "and I've really hesitated to speak a word of it, even to you. I've not whispered it to anyone else. But now you know."

"As you said, though, we *don't* know. We have only the word of Mrs. Brevold. And who knows how reliable *she* is?" Father Lou had somewhat recovered his equilibrium.

"What's to be done? What's to be done?" Philip moaned. "I told her I'd handle it. I believe I may have sworn it – even in *Italian*!"

Father Louis' wit did not fail him now. "At least, then, it was not sworn in *Latin*."

Father Phil was beyond joking. He simply stared morosely into his untouched glass of Pinot Blanc and looked as pale as the forsaken wine.

"What's to be done?" he moaned again, hopelessly.

38

Now Father Lou's professional training was needed, now he could rise above his boss and help him out of his jam. "Why, just act," he said to the pastor.

"Yes, just to act," Louis continued. "First of all we must unearth the true facts, before jumping to any conclusions, certainly before facing Father Williamson with any of these absurd accusations, or inquiring into his motives should any of these charges turn out to be true."

"That's right," Phil said dumbly. "Innocent until proven guilty. No Inquisition in America. Let's get the facts. But how?"

"Easy as ice cream melting in Jamaica," Louis said. It was an old expression of his grandfather's, who had come over from Kingston.

But it wasn't so easy. At first he couldn't think about how it was to be done. Suddenly it became crystal clear.

"I'll do it," he said. "I'll go. I'll watch him and see what's what."

"Suppose he sees you?"

"I'll scout the place out beforehand and find a good hiding place. Where is this clearing? Did Mrs. Brevold say?"

"She did, and gave me very precise directions to it, for she was demanding of me that I appear at the place in the, as she put it, 'omnipotence of my pastoral authority,' catch him in the act, in *flagrante*, and cashier him on the spot. I suppose she would like it if I ripped off his Roman collar and impounded his rosary beads."

"No matter. Tell me where and when and I'll get to the heart of the matter."

Father Louis smiled slightly in secret appreciation of his sophisticated allusion to Graham Greene.

The pastor told him precisely where the field was and explained that the strange act was said to occur just before twilight.

Still, Father Lou put off the action he suggested. Then on the next Monday morning, there was a stern message on the machine for Father Phil: "Lucinda Brevold. Call me back."

"It must be today," he said to Lou just before lunch.

"I assume Mrs. Brevold has skewered you again," Father Lou said. "I'm ready. Today. Why not?"

"Go, please. Go!" Phil said in anguish.

Louis peeked into St. Augustine's Church after lunch and spotted Fred praying there, so he knew that he could reach the clearing and hide himself before his fellow curate could arrive. In a little after a half hour he arrived at a mowed clearing.

Lou drove to the other side of the meadow and parked behind a thick stand of pines where the car could not be seen. He walked back across the field looking for signs of recent activity. Just as he thought, near where the road first emerged into the clearing was a little worn area where Fred must have stood when he batted.

From there he walked back up into the woods and found a place in which he could be well hidden and yet have a view of the field. What made this especially eerie was that he was now doing exactly what the imperial Lucinda had done, spying on Fred's weird performance. Father Lou looked down at his feet, with the uneasy feeling that he might be standing just where she had stood. If Lucinda had been doing something discreditable, wasn't he doing the same? Sure, he was doing it for a good reason, to comfort Father Phil, he told himself. But his feelings remained troubled and he fell into a myriad of reflections about unexamined sins of his own. Then he had another thought. What if Lucinda were hidden somewhere, spying on him while he waited to spy on Fred? These strange woods forced strange thoughts upon him.

Fred did arrive, pretty much on schedule, in his Chevy Blazer. By this time the sun had almost gone down below the surrounding trees and the forest where Father Lou stood was in the deep shadow. Out on the field, twilight glowed.

Lucinda had been right. Louis realized that he had all along assumed she had manufactured the tale. But there it was all coming true.

Fred took a rubber home plate out of the back of the Blazer and placed it next to the worn spot. Then he unfolded a metal contraption and wheeled it 60 feet from the plate. He got a couple of big bags of baseballs and loaded the machine.

Fred lifted out a four-foot statute of the Virgin Mary from the backseat, the same statue that usually graced the left side altar, and carried it far out, more than three hundred feet, to what would be centerfield in a ballpark.

On the way back he clicked on the pitching machine, which was regulated by some sort of timer, and hurried to assume a batting position.

The metallic click of the machine, the whirr of the ball being released, and the crack of Fred's bat sounded together. The ball lifted above the trees where the sunlight blazed on it, and then descended near the statue and bounced lazily in the soft ground about fifteen feet past the Virgin.

40

There was no need of a backstop. Fred never missed a ball, though the machine pitched the balls erratically. Mostly he hit high flies back over the pitching machine toward centerfield. He swung with grim determination and a look of complete concentration on his face. By the time the machine was emptied, Mary was surrounded by a scattering of balls.

The machine continued to click and throw even when empty. Fred walked out and shut if off, then picked up his canvas bags, walked out to gather up the balls, loaded the machine once more and began to bat again.

The twilight darkened. Only the highest of flies caught the light of the sun. From where Lou stood, now chilled with the dampness that arose from the moldering leaves underfoot, he could barely see the white baseballs as they hit the ground and dribbled around the statue. He wondered how Fred could see the pitches to loft them up and out so effortlessly and he expected to see one finally whiz by him and bounce against the tree trunk that served superfluously as a backstop. But this never happened, and with the last ball Fred lifted a very high fly that at its peak gleamed in the sun for a moment before it fell.

Lou followed it down as best he could and saw it bounce near the statue, when by a trick of the last light that broke through a space between the trees the sun flashed on the figure, making it look as if Mary's hands were suddenly lifted from her sides, palms facing upward. But only for a moment. Then the statue was as it always had been.

Darkness fell while Fred walked wearily to centerfield and tenderly carried the statue back in his arms, cradled like an infant. He gathered up the balls, packed all the paraphernalia in the Blazer, and drove off, leaving the woods to Father Lou and darkness.

When Lou came into the living room he found his pastor sitting expectantly, twirling a half-finished aperitif of Dubonnet *blonde* in his hand. He pointed to the bottle on the sideboard.

"Join me, Lou," he said. "Fill me in."

Lou said nothing at first.

"Mrs. Brevold called," Phil noted, "and I assured her that I was in charge and that the 'little matter' – the *little* matter – was being handled. I *could* assure her of that, Louis, couldn't I?"

Louis looked up then, saying inconclusively: "You could say that."

"What do you mean? You're not telling me anything," the pastor snapped somewhat testily. "I'm sorry, Lou. I've had a bad afternoon. I kept thinking that I should have gone out there by myself, or gone with you. Then I'd already know now if there's a problem. Don't keep me in suspense."

Just then Fred came in looking for dinner.

"Hello," he said casually, happily.

Good, Lou thought, he doesn't have any idea he was watched.

As the meal proceeded – slowly, slowly, it seemed – toward the coffee, Father Gardiner barely succeeded in restraining the impulse to ask Fred if he didn't have some errands of mercy to attend to – some sick calls, perhaps? If patience is a virtue, Phil achieved virtue. He smiled sweetly and slowly sipped the strong, chocolaty Mexican coffee as if the evening might last eternally.

Finally, Fred did excuse himself – to bring communion to a sick parishioner.

He left quickly. Further patience would have been a vice. Phil demanded: "Well?"

"I am a little at a loss," Louis began, "but I know you'd want me to get right to the point, so here it is. It's all true – the field, the hitting, the statue – yes, the statue, which I'm sure is now sitting securely again in the side altar. All that Mrs. Brevold says is wholly accurate. Yet, her conclusions seem to me to be wrong. It doesn't look crazy. It just doesn't. The feeling I got was that – well, it was sweet, sweet and innocent. Even, if I can say so, beautiful. But I can't quite explain why this feeling is so strong in me."

Lou had actually surprised himself at his own words. He had expected to say only that there didn't seem to be anything wrong at all if an old ball player wanted to lug equipment out into a forsaken field and re-experience what must have been the thrill of batting practice. Good exercise, too. What's the harm? But when he said that there was something beautiful about watching it, he felt a warm pleasure surge up to his temples. He liked the feeling, and so he said again: "Yes, sweet and beautiful."

"But Lou, Lou, Lou," Phil answered, "We can't have a priest of St. Augustine's hitting fly balls at the Virgin Mary. It does look crazy. It sounds crazy to me. What would I say to the Archbishop if he should come to me and say, 'Oh, by the way Father Gardiner, Mrs. Brevold mentioned to me that one of your curates is playing baseball with the Blessed Mother?' Could I reply with a straight face, 'Of course,

Archbishop Oliveti, but it's quite beautiful. We ought to take a picnic out there one of these days and watch a few innings.' Could I say that?"

Lou laughed out loud, laughed with relief.

"Phil, it's good to see that at least you can joke about it. Yes, why not make a sport of it? Tell Mrs. Brevold what you just told me. Tell the Archbishop, too. I'll back you up."

"Sure, it's a nice thought, but you know I can't say that. I like your attitude, and I'm sure you're right. Fred's ideas are not like ours, but he means well. He's not sophisticated. You know what his sermons are like. But he is a simple soul, and Mrs. Brevold is a – I won't say what she is –"

"And she's attributing intentions to Fred that are far from any he has. He's not crazy."

"He's not sacrilegious."

"Of course not."

They were agreed.

But of course, the problem still remained, even without the intervention of Mrs. Brevold. It really was unthinkable to have a priest making such use of a holy statue, and a rather expensive one at that, carved in a Milanese workshop out of acacia wood and beautifully painted.

The answer was obvious. Both priests knew it. Fred would have to be spoken to. "It" would have to be stopped. The necessity didn't need to be stated.

"How will you do it?" Lou asked.

"You saw it. What would you suggest?"

Lou reflected. He rebelled inwardly at making a decision. He was not the pastor.

"Yes, I saw it. And I'd suggest that you see it too. Then you'll know what to do, I'm sure."

Phil moaned. He didn't want to see the batting exhibition. He wanted Lou to tell him what to do. He wanted Lou to do it.

They sat in silence for ten minutes.

"We'll go together. I'll watch it with you," Phil said at last, resignedly.

"Tomorrow, then?"

Father Gardiner suppressed another moan and replied decisively: "Yes, it must be so."

The worst was over. The future was settled. Fred's batting practice was already consigned to being a mere bump on an otherwise smooth highway.

Father Phil went to his room and watched Fox News, fair and balanced. He began to feel fair and balanced himself. This too, this business of Fred, would pass.

On Tuesday the two priests stood together in Louis's hiding place.

Fred arrived in the same way and grimly completed his preparations.

He had taken no more than a half-dozen swings when Phil and Louis heard a branch crackling behind them, and a little cry of "Ouch," as a dry limb snapped up and hit Lucinda Brevold in the ankle.

"So, I see that at least you are investigating this travesty," she hissed, reaching down to rub her smarting bone.

The two clerics looked at her with astonishment.

"But why do you let him go on? This should stop at once."

Phil literally opposed her for once and put his forefinger to his lips, gesturing and lightly saying, "Shush."

She shushed. But anyone could see that she was straining and steaming inside.

Fred kept swinging in his effortless way. It must have been important to him to hit each ball well, to do it right. Whatever mission he was on, whatever act he was performing, it needed to be done purely, without an error.

The boiler in Lucinda exploded.

"What *are* you going to do? Tell me. Tell me now," she demanded, though still in subdued tones.

The spirit of opposition rose up in Father Gardiner.

"Why not just enjoy the game," he suggested flippantly. "Just look at the grace of his swing."

A phrase came into his mind.

"It's fair and balanced, a beautiful motion."

Lucinda's amazement at the treatment she was receiving, treatment far beneath what she regarded as her due, kept her quiet for a while, until the pitching machine was emptied and Fred picked up the bags to collect the balls from centerfield.

When he was far away, she said in a normal voice, "I demand that you put a stop to this. I won't have it on my land."

44

"But it's not *your* land anymore, Mrs. Brevold," Phil replied. "It belongs to the Estates Corporation now."

"I tell you, I won't have it. It's Brevold land, it's always been Brevold land, it always will be Brevold land, no matter what it says in some bill of sale, and I want this stopped."

So that was it. Father Phil understood that she needed to control everything that happened on this earth. Did she peek into people's windows? Did she creep up on lovers parked in their cars? Did she examine the garbage of the residents during the middle of the night to assure herself that no depravity soiled the land that had been soiled irretrievably when her ancestors cheated the Indians out of these thousands of acres? In her old age, had she appointed herself the guardian of the moral atmosphere of the place and so created the evil that she strained to eliminate?

Fred was back at home plate now, swinging steadily while the light steadily diminished.

He was approaching the end of the balls in the machine, but Lucinda could wait no longer. She stepped out of the circle of trees into plain sight, behind Fred and raised her fist, preparing to speak.

Fred's bat cracked sharply and her eyes, like those of the two priests, automatically fell on the flight of the ball as it sped up in darkness, briefly flashing at its apex, and then descended like a meteor, shedding sparks of light behind it. The three watchers palpably held their breaths, for the ball, for the first time in all of Fred's hits, seemed to be dropping directly toward the statue. And then night nearly enveloped all.

Later on, none of them ever talked about what they saw. But in the last moment before the ball was about to shatter the statue, what Father Lou believed he saw was that the Blessed Mother stepped gracefully off her pedestal and coolly caught the ball. A tiny spark, like a world going out. Then darkness. Of course, this was a trick of the slanting light.

Whatever Lucinda saw made her stagger back without a word, only a little gasp. Backpedaling, she tripped over her own feet and would have crashed to the ground except that Father Phil had rushed out to try and draw her back into the trees, and he now stood a few feet behind her. She fell into his outstretched arms, and for a moment they froze in that position.

Then he hoisted her up. She straightened her dress and composed her face, so that when Phil whispered, "It's finished," she smiled her best smile and said, "Yes." Then both of them retreated back into the woods.

45

For his part, Fred walked toward centerfield to collect the baseballs and the statue, while his audience slipped away.

Just before dinner, Lou walked over to the church. When he returned, he told Phil, "It's back there, same as always."

After the apple pie had been cleared away, Fred went out of the room and came back with his old glove.

"Look at this," he said. "It's my old glove, the golden glove from when I played with the Sox." He brought out his bat too.

For Fred, something was over. He donated the bat and glove to St. Augustine's Fall raffle.

Lucinda Brevold waited until the bidding for the bat and glove reached a two thousand dollar bid by a rabid Red Sox fan. Then she lifted her paddle and offered ten thousand for them.

After all, she explained, it was a wise investment to have the bat and glove of the only priest in American history who would soon make the Hall of Fame.

Fathers Phil and Fred smiled at this.

The Blessed Mother remained rooted like the tree of life to the place on the side altar where she had always been and always would be.

WHY JANE AUSTEN NEVER MARRIED

A Newly Discovered Letter
EDITOR'S INTRODUCTION

Neither R.W. Chapman, in his invaluable collection, *Jane Austen's Letters to Her Sister Cassandra and Others* (Oxford, 1952), nor William and Richard Austen-Leigh in their earlier *Jane Austen : Her Life and Letters. A Family Record* (Smith, Elder, 1913), or even in recent biographies, such as Carol Shields' *Jane Austen* (Weidenfeld and Nicholson, 2001), is any mention made of a letter which was evidently composed at Bath in 1802, not long after Ms. Austen first accepted, and then almost immediately rejected, a proposal of marriage tendered to her by Mr. Harris Biggs-Wither.

Her reasons for this refusal and for the consequence that she was to remain forever unmarried have always remained obscure, though psychological, social, and economic reasons, among many others, have been adduced by such of her biographers as Halpern, Nokes, and Tomalin. That this "new" letter brings some clarity – how much the reader must determine – to this hitherto cloudy issue suffuses it with the most intense interest and highest importance.

How is it, the reader of this account is likely to inquire, that an epistle of such singular importance has remained unnoticed for so long? The reason is easy to state. No scholar before me has seen it. It was pasted onto page 96 of Horatio Smith's *Festivals, Games, and Amusements*, published in London in 1831 by James Cadbury, Printer, of Charing Cross. Being smaller in size than the pages in that volume, the letter would have remained unobserved to all but to someone who paged carefully through the book. In 1831, of course, Jane had been dead for fourteen years, and therefore she herself could not be held responsible for so effectively sequestering the letter. When the Smith's book came up for auction in 1976, with a provenance guaranteeing that it had been owned by a member of the Austen family, it was acquired by an anonymous buyer for the Special Collections library of the University of Edinburgh.

There it rested undisturbed until I sought out the volume to inspect in connection with the forthcoming publication of my *A Catalogue of the Libraries of Jane Austen and Her Family, 1775 to 1840.* I conjecture that one of her descendents discerned a connection between the letter and a passage in Smith's book occurring on page 97 that is faintly

47

underlined in black ink. The underscored passage reads: "…young men are expert in a variety of games of ball – such as cricket, base, cat, football, trapball…." The relevance of this passage to her letter will be easily seen in the reading of it.

The letter is addressed to an unidentified correspondent, called only "Catherine." All women of Jane's known acquaintance named "Catherine" or "Cathy" or "Kate" have been ruled out as possible recipients. Moreover, the tone of the letter, with its abrupt and hardly intimate opening, does not prompt us to believe that this anonymous "Catherine" was among her familiar acquaintance.

The question must arise: was it even sent? Was this "Catherine" a real person or perhaps a mere literary cipher, a device, an *alter ego*, through which Jane reflected on the reasons she refused to wed? The brutal frankness and remarkable openness of the letter forces upon our consideration the possibility that it was never sent because the recipient was no other than herself. Alas, though the answer is perhaps not beyond someday knowing, it is, in the present state of our knowledge, beyond our powers of conclusive speculation as well as the propriety of my editorial task.

I leave all further conjecture to the interested reader.

THE LETTER

A rumor, to which you allude, that I was the grateful recipient of a proposal of marriage from Mr. Harris Biggs-Wither; and that to all appearances I warmly accepted it, only, with equal force, to reject it in a cruel, preemptory manner has, it must be admitted, some glimmer of truth to it as to its facts; for indeed I did accept, then refuse his offer of alliance. But as in all such matters of the emotions, your account is a superficial one with reference to my own attitude in the matter. To society, I admit, my seemingly erratic behavior would suggest a deficiency of resolution along with a changeability most blamable in a woman who has passed out of the wild waters of early girlhood into the serene port and the resolute condition of a mature woman. Indeed, to say the truth, at the date of Mr. Biggs-Wither's proposal I had acquired the mature and sensible age of twenty-six years, well beyond the date when most properly educated young ladies have settled their affections upon a suitable partner and given a consent to his entreaties. That I did not do so gives you no warrant, to be sure, to inquire into my motives, but as your query has brought forcefully and painfully to my mind the circumstances of the reversal of a sentimental promise, I find myself undeniably obliged to examine my motives and to speak for myself.

I begin my account, so it would seem to anyone besides myself, far from the question at hand. First of all, I must confess to being a writer of books, a scribbler of novels. Of course, by the date of Mr. Biggs-Wither's appearance as a suitor, no one outside the little circle of my family and a few of my dearest friends even suspected that I was addicted to composition. Sketching, playing at the pianoforte, sewing, and the like were certainly accepted and considered to be pleasing activities for a young lady who sought correct manners to pursue. A moderate devotion to religious services and a just regard for the beneficial effects of rationally reverent attitude were known to be becoming and most properly thought to promote personal tranquility and to prophesy a capacity for creating domestic felicity for herself, her husband, and the children who would be raised in the bosom of the happiness that a good wife would create and sustain.

But a lady, no longer in the prime of her life, who had become addicted to scribbling, this was an aberration not lightly to be ignored. For seven years, I had toiled away at my compositions. Whole books, books of sufficient length to attain to the brink of three or four volumes, had already flowed from my pen. To the world at large, being unpublished, I was known only as well-mannered and agreeable Jane Austen, but to the small audience for my tales, I was the author of "Elinor and Marianne," "First Impressions," and "Susan."[1]

This is the mixed state in which Mr. Biggs-Wither discovered me. When I first noticed that in him strong affections towards me were undeniably appearing, I took him at once into my confidence and spread before him the several mighty manuscripts to which I had already given birth, along with outlines for yet more weighty tomes to come.

He was astonished. But I was delighted to see that he soon actually commenced to take some small interest in my authorial offspring and even ventured to beg permission to peruse some of it. If I was, so to speak, the strangest fish he had even pulled from a stream, to him I was at least a particularly interesting instance of the scaled vertebrates. To my mind, my literacy enthusiasms, indeed my avowed vocation as an author, might offer insuperable objections to the kind of marriage that a

---

[1] Editor's note: these were the early titles of *Sense and Sensibility*, *Pride and Prejudice*, and *Northanger Abbey*.

person of Mr. Biggs-Wither's personal taste and class conviction would desire.

I was wrong. He proposed to read my pages. He read. And he saw in them no reason to defer a matrimonial proposal.

"Jane," he said at the decisive moment, "You write blessedly well, and I have always held that good writing means clear thinking, and clear thinking implies careful morals, and fine morals are the indispensable element of a splendid wife."

"Mr. Biggs-Wither," I replied, "I am deeply impressed. I find myself amazed at the breadth of your conceptions, even as at the same moment I expected no less of you. You are an excellent man."

"Of course, Jane, I am no judge of fiction, for I daresay I have read but one novel, *The Vicar of Wakefield*, but take me as I am. I like your compositions, and like you even more."

"Do you conceive, then," I asked, "that you would have no objection, were we to be married, for me to continue on my course, writing with the hope of eventual publication and the aim of assisting my family financially – not, of course, in a way that would conflict with my domestic duties and my devotion to you, but writing, yes, writing incessantly."

"Bless me," he replied. "Only a few men these days talk about incessant labor. I am deeply impressed by your fervor, even if its object is merely to fill the shelves of stationer's shops."

"I must assume, then, that you perceive no conflict between the duties of a wife and her devotion to writing."

"Surely, none. You may amuse yourself to your heart's content, and even publish, should the opportunity arise, so long as the ascription is an anonymous one."

Our discourse on the matter of authorship having reached a natural terminus to my entire satisfaction, I declared myself, as he entreated me to do, more than content to marry.

Mr. Biggs-Wither departed. I made haste to my room with the idea for a new novel which, should I eventually write it, will concern a family named Watson.

On mid-morning of the following day, my now betrothed suitor returned to pledge his devotion and more specifically, to bid me farewell until he should return in a fortnight's time from a pressing matter of business.

To my surprise, he continued to speak of my writings; to be precise, of my most recently completed manuscript.

"So pleased was I," he began, "with our conversation last evening that I picked up "Susan," which is, I believe, your latest, but I am sure not your last foray. Perusing it and seeing the necessity for some small alterations in it, I suddenly grasped how splendid it would be, Jane, for me to take an occasional holiday from the press of business and assist you in improving the taste and correctness of your texts. A man's opinion, I am convinced, could greatly improve the taste in your narratives."

I was thunderstruck. "My correctness? My taste?" was all I could mutter.

"Yes, yes," he pressed on eagerly, "together we shall spread before the public novels that will contribute to the public good."

"But, sir," I said weakly, "what in heaven's name do you mean?"

"Only your welfare, dear Jane."

"I beg of you," I humbly said, though not at all feeling humble, "do give me an instance where my taste is faulty. I shall be glad, by any means, to improve my style or alter my perspective."

"Gladly," he replied, beaming with the glow of a sunny benevolence.

He produced the manuscript from his satchel and placed it on a nearby table, then turned over a few pages until he reached a paragraph which he considered to be cursed with a blemish. He poked the offending passage rudely with his forefinger.

"Here, look here," he fairly shouted. "I'll read it to you."

"Do so at once, I beg you," I said with apprehension.

"In introducing the Morland family, you create a person who is unnatural, most unnatural. Listen."

He read my own words to me.

'Mrs. Morland was a very good woman...' "I skip a bit here," Mr. Biggs-Wither said, '...but her time was so much occupied that her elder daughter was inevitably left to shift for herself; and it was not very wonderful that Catherine, should prefer cricket...and baseball to books.'

"Mind you," Mr. Biggs-Wither added, "this Catherine is said to be already fourteen years old."

"Why, Mr. Biggs-Wither, what can you mean by reading me this passage?"

"Do you not see, Jane, that you can only give scandal to the public and damage to your own character should you ever put into print such an ill model of womanhood as this? Do you not see, to say it plainly, she defies nature? Bless me, a girl of fourteen who prefers play at boys' games rather than acquiring an education in morals and manners from a

51

judicious period of reading a selection of sensible books properly suited to feminine nature. It is not correct, it is not tasteful, to offer the public such a model. You would be much blamed were you to do so. To be sure, I understand that the likelihood of your scribblings ever being printed is small. You told me, did you not, you offered 'First Impressions' to a publisher, but that he refused it forthwith. Still, in these vulgar days, once anything is written down, who knows if it may be printed? Think how your own name would be subjected to public calumny; and, were we to be married, my name as well. Why, by your own account you are a lover of books, and the prospective author of the very thing scored by this roguish Catherine."

He paused. I said nothing, of which he was glad, for he seemed to conclude that I was exhibiting a cordial submission, and besides, puffed up as he was by his air of polite rectitude, he had not yet expelled all of his fusty nonsensical airs, but had still more advice to render.

"Fortunately, I am here to call such deviations from decency to your appreciative attention. Indeed, I have made a list of all the passages to which our attention should be forcefully drawn, and when time permits I shall do the same for your other productions."

To be blunt, I saw that the man I had just yesterday engaged to marry was a complete dunce. I was compelled to speak not.

"Mr. Biggs-Wither, you say you have read my tale of the Morlands through and through. Do you not see that it portrays a family very like my own, and that Catherine is very like myself?"

"Not at all. I see nothing of the sort. You are a sensible woman, whilst she is the very spirit of rebellion, defying her years, her station, her gender, her family and nature itself, incorrect in every way. She is the epitome of *contra naturum*."

I found myself beyond exasperation.

"Then, sir, you do not know me. I am Catherine. I have played cricket and round-ball and cat and base. I did indeed prefer these games to books."

"I am astonished to hear you say so, Jane."

"Then be prepared to be astonished still further. I tell you frankly that though I have just now expressed my pleasure in ball games in the past tense, I must shift to the present, for I still am devoted to these games, and base-ball most especially. As I told you yesterday, I am committed to compositions. But I must state further that now, though I am twenty-six and no longer fourteen, I still prefer ball games to books, yes, even to my own books. Writing, it may be, is to be my vocation, but playing base-ball is my avocation, my dearest pleasure."

Now it was Mr. Biggs-Wither's turn to be thunderstruck. His mouth gaped. I think his eyes rolled.

"But," he gasped, "but – you – do not play –?"

"I do indeed, sir. This very day I expect to play a delicious game of base. With boys."

"I have been very mistaken in you. I regarded you as a person of sense, but I see now that a wild sensibility reigns in you."

His feelings seemed to be injured, and he behaved as if I had intended to hurt him.

"Mr. Biggs-Wither," I said with regained composure, "this has been an enlightening conversation we have had today. As gratifying as our agreement was yesterday, today's discourse is yet more gratifying, for yesterday we allowed ourselves to be deluded into believing we were in accord, while today we have grasped the profound differences between us. For myself, and I hope for you, I am glad of both days' talks."

"But Jane, I was so full of hope after yesterday's agreement and now I am dashed into an abyss."

"Well said," I replied. "But this will pass. Your nature will rise again to the bubbling surface like a cork, and you will, I am sure, discover still greater hope and more full satisfaction in another most fortunate person. I expect that this will not take a long time."

"So, we are not to be joined?"

"It is for the best. Let us part friends. And quickly, since I am due to take the field in a quarter of an hour."

In fact, he had no inclination to linger. Even before he left I could see that his natural sunniness was reviving.

I believe I shall never marry. In my affections, base ball will always have first place, books second, my family next, and society in all its varieties after. It would be disagreeable for a man to be listed seventh in my pleasures.

I hope, Catherine, that you can now understand this matter and if not approve, at least accept, my actions in it.

The only other personal note that I might add is that I am now determined to sell the manuscript of "Susan" to a publisher and to see it printed, especially with the passage in it that offended my suitor so bitterly. If a publisher like Crosby will pay me ten or fifteen pounds for it, I will gladly give it to him.

CONCLUDING NOTE

The letter is signed in Jane Austen's hand, the paper is the same as used in other letters of hers written in 1802-3, and the ink, too, is hers. The authenticity of the letter cannot be doubted.

Jane Austen lived another fifteen years after the date of this epistle. She did sell "Susan" to Crosby in 1803 for £10, but he did not have it printed, and in 1816, she bought the manuscript back from him. However, she died in 1817, and it was not until the next year that "Susan" was published under the title *Northanger Abby*.

Following the publication of my *Catalogue*, it is my intention to explore the relevance of her love of sport, and especially base ball, to the structure and style of her works. Order, the rule of law, an adherence to tradition, suspense as to the outcome, a ritual seriousness, and the drama of a continuous contest and conflict, are all characteristics of both base ball and her novels, as I shall show in a book tentatively titled *Her First Love – Base Ball: A Biographical Key Into the Novels of Jane Austen*.

THE EDITOR

A NEW LIFE

Dr. Alan Washington was always in his office by 7:45 a.m. Detroit was having a welcome mild spell in late October. For ten minutes he examined the notes left for him by the psychiatric social worker concerning those patients who had been brought in overnight, courtesy of the Detroit Police Department. Family members were dithering in reception. At 7:55 he poked his head into the office of Gail Brown, the social worker who did triage.

"See you in the consulting room," Alan said crisply as he glanced at his watch, "in exactly two minutes."

At precisely 8:00 a.m. Gail Brown brought Dr. Washington his first patient of the day. No more than a glimpse of the heavily bandaged left arm of the man was needed.

"Tell me about it," Washington suggested mildly.

The man had a little speech all prepared.

"Doc, believe me, it was just an accident. I was just cutting something and the knife slipped. It just slipped. I feel really bad about troubling my wife and the police and everybody in the Emergency Room with just a stupid accident. All's I want is to get back to the kids. They were kind of screaming and upset, and I just got to get out of here soon as possible for the kids' sakes, and my job."

Washington bent his head toward Gail, who whispered a sentence in his ear.

"Yes, I know you're upset. Of course you want to reassure your family. Forty two stitches is quite a big accident."

He looked at the notes now.

"It seems that you cut deeply into your arm through an artery, nearly to the bone. There must have been lots of blood."

"I guess there was, Doc. I just fainted soon as the accident happened. My old lady and the kids were crying terrible. But I didn't wake up until I was already stitched up. Maybe I remember the paramedics, though, a little."

"You know, if your wife hadn't tied something tight around your arm and held her hand at the crook of your elbow and if the paramedics hadn't come so rapidly, you might have died."

"Gee, that would have been a terrible accident, doc, to leave her and the kids and all alone like that. Got to get back to work, eh?"

"What kind of work do you do?"

"Delivery. Sure, I'm a box delivery man."

55

"Working?"

"Laid off a while back. But I got a job lined up."

"You won't be doing any driving or lifting with that arm," Washington noted.

"But I got to get out, doc. Have a heart. I can't stay in this place."

The same old story. A man could have momentary courage (stupidity, audacity, wildness, whatever one calls it) to thrust a knife through an artery in order to kill himself. Yet, when it came to facing the horror of a psychiatric unit, he'd whimper like a baby.

"You must have been pretty sad about some things, Mr. O'Donnell," Washington stated.

"Oh, I'm all right. I got my head straight now. Can't I go home?"

"Do you know that the police came here with the paramedics and that you have been placed here on a seventy-two hour hold?"

"Why did they do that? Ah, geez," the man groaned. The unshaven stubble stood out blue on his pale face.

"Mrs. Brown is going to talk to your wife, who has been sitting outside for some time now with two sleeping children. I want to send them home with the assurance that social services will be available to them. Mrs. Brown will make the proper referrals to help your family along. You are going to stay with us for at least three days, and very likely more. We'll get you on a good course of medication. I am going to get you started right now."

Washington jotted some notes for the nurses and the attending physician in the ward.

"And I will see you later myself. You can't just go around sticking butcher knives in yourself, can you?"

O'Donnell was taken out by the orderly. He looked as if he had been given a life sentence in the loony bin chamber of horrors.

"I feel sorry for his wife and kids," Gail said.

"Sure. But they've probably had a bad time. Check if there has been any abuse and get a caseworker on it if there was. They'll get a breather without him."

8:37. The next patient arrived. A gauze patch covered his left eye.

"Well, what happened to you?" Washington asked brightly, upbeat.

"Shit happened, that's what."

"Looks like you took a bad beating."

"Took about five guys to get me down. They'll get theirs, don't you worry."

56

"The police report says that you were in the Kon Tiki Bar at 2:00 a.m. Drinking a lot. Your blood alcohol was 1.6. And the fight – it was over a woman?"

"The bitch," he said, "she plays up to me when her man's in the john, and then when he comes out she says, like cum wouldn't melt in her mouth, 'Lester, this stranger's been coming on to me whiles you was in the bathroom.'

"So I say to him, 'Your whore isn't my style. I wouldn't come on to her if she was the last ho twitching her ass in Detroit.'"

"'You calling my girl a ho?'" he asks.

"'If she says I played her, I am,' I say, 'and if she's your girl, then you're a homother.'"

"'Oh yeah,' he shouts, and shoves the highball glass he's holding into my eye."

"You'll get treatment for your injuries here, and some meds to calm you down. I see that your next of kin is your mother. We'll contact her and she'll be able to have a visit with you after a few days. We'll see how it goes. For the time being, you'll be here for the seventy-two hour hold."

He went away cursing Washington.

9:18 a.m. In his office Alan wrote up his two evaluations and treatment plans. Such phrases as "Clinical Depression," "Masochistic ideation," "Dysthymic disorder," "Borderline personality," "Suicidal," "Impulse disorder," "Aggressive acting out syndrome," and "Schizophrenic" flowed into evaluations of these two.

At 10:20 a.m. he opened the locked door of the unit, and went inside. The patients in the sunroom were watching television intently and most paid no attention to his entrance. But the instant that one man who was sitting by the window caught sight of him he hurried over to the doctor.

"Good morning, Mr. Lazzaro," Washington said. "How are you today?"

"I'm wonderful," he answered. "How could I not be as happy as a lark? Our therapeutic sessions have been doing me a world of good."

"That's fine, Peter. I believe I have you down for this afternoon at 3:00 o'clock."

"That's right. I'm looking forward to it. But, Doctor Washington, couldn't we have just a tiny session right now? I had the thought this morning that with just one more session with you I'd be completely cured. You are a miracle worker."

57

Peter Lazzaro had been having this same thought each morning of over three months.

"Peter," Washington said, "we're making progress, I'm sure. But perhaps you still have a way to go before striking out on your own. How long have you been in here, do you remember?"

Peter answered with supreme confidence; "Certainly I do. One thousand fourteen hundred years and seven days. You know that. You were here when I was placed in this dungeon by a witch. But with your help her spell, powerful as it is, will soon be broken."

"We'll persevere," Washington replied. "I want to talk to the staff to be sure you are taking your meds. You wouldn't think of cupping them in your hand and dropping them down your sleeve, would you?"

"The pills they give me are part of the spell," he said. "They keep me crazy."

"We'll talk about that this afternoon."

Washington continued over to a table where a young man was doing a cardboard jigsaw puzzle.

"Mr. Lanham, why don't you follow me into the room over there?" Washington suggested. Lanham complied in a dazed manner.

In the side room, after they took chairs, Washington started: "Mr. Lanham, I admitted you to this unit over two weeks ago now. Since then you broke a nurse's jaw when she tried to give you your medication. You refuse to speak a word to me. Why?"

Frank Lanham stared at the table.

"Is there something that you see on the table top that keeps you from speaking?"

Washington's guess unlocked Lanham's speech.

"Now you know," he said.

"Yes," Washington encouraged him. "Of course I understand that there are secret signs and messages that warn you to be quiet. Will you tell me what they are?"

"You know what they are or you wouldn't ask."

"They are messages that tell you not to give up the great secret?"

"Of course. We know that."

"Yes, let's share the secret."

"The secret is" – Frank looked ominous – "that if I tell the secret" –

"Yes, I know."

– "The world will turn to shit."

"Ah, to shit." Washington did not ask this as a question.

"Complete shit."

58

"Everywhere."

"Yes, everything."

"But Frank, you have told the secret and the world has not turned to shit, has it?"

"I did not tell. You knew it already. But for all we know the real world may have turned to shit. Where we're talking, we wouldn't know if the real world had turned to shit."

Washington said, "We've made good progress today, Frank, I have an idea that we can avert the disaster if we work together."

"Paranoid schizophrenic," he wrote in his notepad.

11:20 a.m. Washington decided to make one more evaluation before breaking for lunch.

The man who was brought in showed no visible signs of bodily injury.

"Why are you here?" Alan asked quietly. "I don't have a file for you."

"To tell the truth, I don't know."

He was wearing an Indian blanket bathrobe over pajamas.

"Could you tell me your name?" Alan asked.

"Al." He stuck out his hand, but Alan didn't tale it. "Al Singer."

"You were brought in by the police?"

"Yes, I was. But I don't know why they brought me here."

"Could you try to guess?" Alan inquired.

"I suppose they made a mistake."

"Sometimes they do. Perhaps you could tell us what they accused you of doing."

"Well I suppose they thought I was damaging my wife's car."

"Were you?"

"No."

"Were you doing some damage to a car?"

"Yes."

"What were you doing?"

"I was trying to smash it to pieces with a baseball bat. This is not an easy thing to do. In fact, as I found out, it's really impossible to do. Cadillacs are really put together well here in Detroit. I'm sure you've never tried to smash a car into bits doctor, but let me tell you, it's one helluva job."

"And so you were smashing your wife's or, as you say, trying to do so, but failing."

"No."

59

"No?"

"No."

"Why not?"

"It's my car in the first place. And in the second place I'm not married. She's my girlfriend. They thought she was my wife."

"Why did they think so?"

"She told them she was."

"So the police got everything wrong?"

"I was smashing my car. I believe that in the US of A, somebody can smash his own car to smithereens if he wants to. I'm free, white, and twenty-one. Pardon me, doctor, I mean no insult to you."

"No insult taken. But I'd like to hear why you were smashing your own car."

"Looking back on it, it's sort of hard to tell. Now it seems stupid. But what the heck, it's just a car. I can always get another one. All I can tell you is I was so worked up that when I picked up my bat I just wanted to smash something. I wanted to smash her, but I knew I shouldn't. So I ran outside. And when the first swing shattered the windshield it was so sensational and it felt so swell that I swung again. Then there's my girlfriend screaming out the window, 'My husband wants to kill me, he's crazy, he's beating my car. Somebody call the police.' So I shouted at her, 'Yeah, you're driving me crazy. Watch this!' And I gave the Caddy another good jolt."

Alan said nothing. The man continued.

"Doc, give me your opinion. I doubt, actually, that I'll need a new car. It's probably just bodywork. I bet the engine and tranny are still tip-top. What do you think?"

"I prefer to ask the questions," Washington replied rather testily. Don't let them take over, he told himself.

"Okay, fire away," the fellow said affably.

"You were arguing about – ?"

"I suddenly realized that she was crazy, completely nuts. I've only known her for a month, and even so I've been out of town a lot. At first she seemed just kind of daffy, but exciting. She moved herself in while I was on the road last time. There she was when I came back. She's kind of cute and she likes to say she's my wife, but she isn't, and calls herself Lauren Singer when she answers the phone. But yesterday she was really out of line. She got me so frustrated I was beside myself."

"So, she is the crazy one?"

"Sure, and if I stayed with her she'd drive me nuts too."

60

"You must have had good reason to believe that she was disturbed."

"Disturbed! That's an understatement. She says that every time I play in a game, an invisible sorcerer is actually doing my playing and setting the records. I'm not doing it. I don't deserve the credit. It's The Other that's doing all the work. She just calls him The Other – like in capital letters: THE OTHER. Gives me the shivers. And then to top it off, she says to me, 'I've kept this a secret from you, but I might as well tell you since it will soon be revealed' – she talks like that in a spooky way – 'it will soon be revealed – so you should know from my lips. Every time you go out of town THE OTHER stays here with me, and we spend all day long making hot love. The OTHER just keeps doing me and doing me all day and all night, and even when I'm exhausted and try to hide in a closet or under the bed, he finds me out and does me again. That's why I'm so worn out when you get home.' Doc, if that isn't crazy, what is?"

"So you believe you set records in the games you play?"

"Yes, I do."

"And what games do you play?"

"Just one. Baseball. I'm a big star."

"You play for?"

"The Detroit Tigers, of course. Why else would I be living in this town?"

"Well, Mr. Singer, we'll talk more about those things later. I'm truly interested in your case."

"You want a great case, get Laureen. You should hear the weird things she says."

"I'm sure I will. Try to relax. You'll be with us for at least three days."

"Okay by me, if the bed is comfortable. Anyways, if I left here where would I go? She's in my apartment, probably cutting up the sheets. I can't go back there till she clears out. Do you think she'll wander off in three days time?" he asked, innocently as a child.

Dr. Washington was scribbling some notes and didn't look up.

He gave directions to Luis, the orderly.

"Mr. Calderon will find a nice comfortable bed for you. And there's television and jigsaw puzzles, and tomorrow afternoon we have art therapy with Dr. Stone. Nurse will give you some pills to take in a paper cup and you'll be sure to take them, eh?"

"Why not. Sounds ok to me. I can use a little sane company."

After lunch, Alan passed Luis in the hall.

61

"Man, do you know who that guy could be, Dr. Washington?" Luis asked, awestruck.

"Who?"

"Yeah, he's Al Singer."

"That's the name he gave us and the police. So?"

"Al Singer. Don't you know? Plays for the Tigers."

Calderon seemed a little impatient with Alan's ignorance of local sports.

"Sure. The Detroit Tigers."

"You say Mr. Singer plays baseball? *This* Mr. Singer?"

"I dunno. Where I sit in the bleachers, you can't see faces real clear. This guy in here could be anybody, Joe Schmoe. Maybe just thinks he is Al Singer. But he does look a little like the pictures in the paper."

Washington went into the ward to see his newest patient.

"So," he said soothingly, "you are Al Singer?"

He expected to hear a new story, have a new identity pop out.

But the patient merely said, "Sure am."

Dr. Washington knew that he was dealing with a grandiose delusion, but he played along with it, as he had been taught to do in his psychiatric residency.

"And who is Al Singer?"

"Don't you read the papers? Maybe docs are too busy. Al Singer, the Allstar Zinger. Al Singer, the One Base Swinger. You know, the Detroit Tigers guy who just this season broke Joe DiMaggio's record of hitting in fifty-six straight games. *That* Al Singer. Me."

"And in how many consecutive games did you make a hit?"

"Sixty-nine. A full thirteen more than Old Joe. But," he added, "Old Joe did set a record I can't break. He married Marilyn Monroe, the hottest woman ever in the world. Those years must have been incredible for the old Bronx Bomber. All I get is a ditzy dame with corn flakes for brains."

Alan noticed but ignored the man's preoccupation with sex. Sixty-nine straight games, Marilyn Monroe.

"It's quite a feat to set a record."

"Lot's of luck and a clear eye. It could have busted anytime along the way. The old record lasted for more than sixty years. The last big old timers' hitting record to be topped. How long do you think my record will stand?"

Dr. Washington didn't take the bait.

"I gather you're pleased about it."

"Records are records, they're meant to be broken. But I get to re-up my contract for beaucoup bucks. Besides, my agent says that it looks like I'm to join the line of greats featured on boxes of Wheaties. Me and Tiger Woods. And *that's* money. It all starts flowing in."

"So why were you so upset about Laureen?"

"Doc, did you forget already? I sort of told you. First of all, when I picked up the baseball bat I thought, wow, I'm going to hit something – but I don't want to start with flesh and blood. So I look around. There's nothing in the apartment to smash. Then I think, yesterday I told Laureen I was going to get a new car with all the money coming in, something grand, and I'd give her my year-old Caddy. So when she's frustrating me like crazy with all her spooky talk, I say to her 'If you don't shut up and stop cutting up all the sheets, sure I'll give you that car I promised you – because I don't go back on promises – but I'm going to wreck it first.' So she sasses me and says, 'Yeah, then I'll get THE OTHER to smash you up worse.' That did it. I'm in my PJs and bathrobe but I'm so nuts with her antics that I rush outside just meaning to give it a tap. But she starts in the screaming, and to show her, I get into the flailing of the bat."

"I see," Washington said, anxious to get back to his office and write down all this juicy material.

"Dr. Washington, I was thinking. I guess I'm ready to get out of here after all if that's ok with you. I don't want to be any trouble."

"You were admitted only a few hours ago, my friend. It's too soon. Relax."

"I know you're concerned about me. And sure, I know you think I was a little over the edge, too much excitement what with setting the record and all. But I don't have to go to the apartment if Laureen's still there. I can bunk with Sid Long – he's another outfielder. You go to the Tigers' games sometimes, don't you? You might know him, he's African-American too. And if not Sid, there's always hotels. I'll consult my agent. You don't have to worry about me, you'll see. After all, I'm not crazy now like I was."

All psychotics contend they are perfectly sane, of course.

"I haven't even had a chance to examine your file. We'll just start there. How does that sound to you?"

"That's swell. I could use a nap. Maybe they have a sleeping pill in that little cup. A little snooze would do me the world."

7:45 a.m. the next day, Dr. Alan Washington was back in his office. At precisely 7:58 he looked into Gail Brown's office. "See you in the consulting room in exactly two minutes," he said crisply.

At 8:00, Gail brought Dr. Washington his first patient.

"Good morning," he started. "How can I help you?"

Before him sat a sullen young woman. She said nothing.

"You must not have gotten much sleep," he guessed. "You look tired. What time were you brought here?"

Nothing. No answer.

"Do you know where you are?"

No reply.

"This is the Psychiatric Emergency Admitting Ward of Metropolitan Hospital. You were brought here by the police so that we can make a judgment about whether it will be safe for you and society to return you to your home. You have to help us to do that. Let me introduce myself. I am Dr. Alan Washington."

He nodded towards Gail and Luis.

"I am Mrs. Brown. Tell me how to contact your family."

"Luis Calderon."

"All right," Washington said, "now will you introduce yourself and tell us something about you?"

"What will happen to me if I tell my name?" she asked suspiciously.

"Then we can get to know you better."

Her eyes glared. "Know me? I know what you mean. You mean sex. I'm Martha, Dr. Washington. Screw me." Then she began to scream: "My name is Lollypop, lollypop, lollypop!"

She lunged toward him. "Lollypop! SUCK ME, Dr. Washington!" She stuck her tongue out at him and rolled her eyes.

Luis held her by her shoulders from behind.

"Dr. Washington," Gail said quickly. "I have her file. Her name is Laureen." –

"Laureen lollypop. SUCK ME, Luis!" the woman was shouting. "I know what you want. And you lady" – starting at Gail – "You don't care, you don't count. You're a lesbian."

"Laureen," Mrs. Brown continued, "was brought in from the same address as the young man we saw yesterday, Mr. Singer."

Something was going cold in Alan.

"She told the police that she is married to Mr. Singer and her name is Laureen Singer."

"Why is she here?" Alan asked weakly.

"The police report says she was throwing everything belonging to Mr. Singer out of the window of the apartment which he owns in his name only – signed baseballs, a bat, his clothes, dishes – everything. She was scattering cut-up pieces of red satin sheets from the window, like confetti at Mardi Gras. Several neighbors complained. She tried to injure the policeman who brought her in, I gather, by kneeing him in the groin."

"I don't care, do anything!" Laureen was shouting. "Do ME!" Two orderlies came into the room. Head nurse Sara followed. Gail had pushed the "stat" button in the consultation room.

"Do it all," she hissed. "I've had it from the best! No one can do it like THE OTHER. You can't bother me."

Sara gave her an injection in her left arm.

Laureen shouted, "Yes, stick it in. Do me again. Tell Al he's out of my life, I've thrown him out."

She looked suspiciously at them. "You know Al, don't you? Thinks he broke records, does he? You tell him for me, we're through. No," she smiled triumphantly, "he's through. He never was no good."

She sagged. Sara and Luis helped her through the door. At the same moment the Hospital Administrator came through it from the other direction.

"Dr. Washington," she said hurriedly. "I've just received a most distressing phone call from the owner of the Detroit Tigers baseball franchise. It seems that we have their star outfielder, who just set a new record for hitting in sixty-nine straight games, in our locked ward. Do you know something about this?" She took a breath and continued: "And on my way down here I was told that there is a crowd of reporters and photographers and who knows what out in the reception room wanting to see somebody. I suppose that means me."

"Reporters?" Alan whispered.

"And a lawyer with a show-cause order why Albert Singer should not be discharged immediately, a police lieutenant with a discharge of a seventy-two hour hold in his hand, two other attorneys who are shouting threats about false arrest and false incarceration, an attorney representing the Tigers franchise, a sports agent who is talking about a seven-figure suit if this gets out and a contract with Kellogg's Wheaties falls through. And, at last count, seven reporters and eight cameramen. In the time it's taken me to say this, the crowd has probably doubled....Dr. Washington, what are you going to do about this?"

65

Alan felt the sands of a twenty-two year career shifting under his feet. He had done his best. He had been faithful in taking all his continuing medical education credits. He had read the journals. He had had a good two-year psychoanalysis by an eminent practitioner in Birmingham. He had published a paper on the work of Otto Kernberg. He always studied the PDR when considering new medications. What more could he have done?

"Do?" he asked.

"Yes. To me will fall the odious task of going out into that raging mob and handling the public reaction."

"And I?"

"You will go to Mr. Singer to try to soothe whatever anger he may be experiencing at being unjustly locked up, and humble yourself, if necessary, with the most profound apologies. If you don't succeed —"

She let it go at that.

And left.

Alan stood up in a daze of information-overload.

Singer was not in his bed.

Singer was not milling around the nurses' station.

He found Al in the television room. He seemed to be talking to Pete Lazzaro. He was not at all agitated.

"Mr. Singer," Alan began.

The ballplayer leaped to his feet.

"Doc, how ya doin'?"

"I'm fine," Alan answered spontaneously. Without thinking he had answered a patient's question.

"I've come to see you."

"No problem," Al said, "I've been whiling away the morning chattering with Pete here."   "We're pals," Lazzaro put in.

Washington said, "I'd like to speak to you in private. It's a matter of some urgency." He motioned toward a side room.

"Let's do it. See ya in a while, Pete," Al called.

"Okay, Al."

"That Pete is a nice guy except that he talks endlessly about some witch as if I know about her. But he sure thinks the world of you, Doctor Washington. He says you're the best head shrinker anywhere and that you're bringing him back to life."

"Nice of him to say so," Alan said. He stumbled toward an apology.

"It seems that there had been a mistake. The police – …Well, not a mistake exactly. But there are some friends of yours waiting outside and I want to release you to them immediately."

"You mean, leave?"

"Yes, leave."

"Let me tell you the truth, Doctor Washington. I thought a lot about it overnight. And I saw how I've been off the beam, what with all the tension of the hitting streak. I didn't know it was getting to me so much, but it must have been. And so I got involved with that dipstick Laureen. And then I really went wild and was bashing my own Caddy. Last night, I told myself, 'Al, my boy, you can't go on this way. You got another ten, twelve years of big league ball left in you if you get your head straight.'"

"Good, good," Alan urged him.

"And then I got to talking to Pete there, and believe me he's got plenty of stories about you that would make Sigmund Freud blush. And so I changed my mind from yesterday when I asked to leave. The season's over. I thought I'd just stay here a month or two and let you shrink me. What about it?"

"God, no," Alan said, feeling a cold shiver. "I've got to get you released right away. There's a mob clamoring for you in the reception room."

"That's just it," Al said in a pleading way. "Out there, someone always wants a piece of you, an interview, a photo, an autograph – it goes on and on. Here today, I'm starting to feel at peace. I'm ready to do whatever you say to keep that good feeling going. Tell me to repeat 'Om' a thousand times and it's jake by me. Whatever you say, I'm your man."

"But it's impossible. No one wants to stay in the locked ward."

"See, doc, that means I must be crazy. You sure got me there. I refuse to go."

"You must go."

"I'm not going anywhere that I might have to face that dippy broad Laureen."

Dr. Washington saw his opening.

"But Laureen's here," he said.

"*Here?*"

"In the hospital."

"Then, I'm not *that* crazy to stay where she's around. I'm leaving."

"Just follow me," Alan said, relieved.

67

Singer followed him until they reached the reception room door.

When Al Singer said at the door, "But how will I keep my head straight without you?" Alan had an inspiration.

"I've been thinking of starting a private practice in Birmingham. Call me!"

He thrust a card into Al's hand and pushed him out the door, into the maelstrom.

It was a true vision. He'd start with Al Singer, then branch out and become a full-fledged sports psychiatrist. Do the Tigers, then take on whole teams all across the country. Fame and fortune would follow. He would be free at last.
A new life.

9:37 a.m. For the first time in his career, Dr. Alan Washington decided to knock off after only on hour and thirty-seven minutes of work. He took off his wristwatch and locked it in his desk drawer.

RECONSTRUCTION

I was born the day the Civil War ended, April 9, 1865. My father was a colonel in the Union army. Up to that time the most notable event in his life was that in 1860 he played second base when Columbia beat New York University in the first intercollegiate baseball game in American history.

He stayed in the army at the war's end. So I grew up helter-skelter in the West among roustabouts and ruffians, Indians, settlers, immigrants, and cowboys in remote forts and unsettled regions. Then, when I was eleven, we were posted to the South, to Jefferson, the county seat of Yoknapatawpha County, Mississippi. This town had, as my mother remarked, at least some "elements of civility." Certainly, there were sometimes knife fights on the streets, duels in secluded places, drunken brawls, dirt-poor farmers, prostitutes, genteel romantics still dazed by defeat in the war, merchants barely scraping through, and land grabbers on the make. But there were also men and women who had once traveled to Europe and spoke several languages beside Choctaw and Cree. Old General Compson wasn't the only one there who read Latin. So did the mayor of the town, Robert Johnson, who had attended Yale College because his idol, John C. Calhoun, had gone there.

While my father and mayor Johnson had been on opposite sides in the war they had the common bond that both had gone to northern schools. A second bond was that both had played baseball in college. During the war all soldiers played the game, even in the prison camps.

In Jefferson the Union soldiers soon made a diamond adjacent to their barracks, while the townspeople had laid out a separate, more permanent field near the town center.

My father had been posted to Jefferson to make sure that the South was "reconstructed" – meaning that the black population would not be reduced once more to slavery. Trouble was, reconstruction was almost worn out when we got there. By the summer of 1876 all the talk was about the upcoming presidential election between Hayes and Tilden. "If Tilden wins," my father announced at the dinner table, "the Civil War would have been fought in vain." Then the election's result was uncertain. We waited for the disputed election to be decided.

"It is obvious, William," Mayor Johnson said to my dad, "that the election will be declared for Tilden. Reconstruction will end. You'll be out of a job."

"Reconstruction must continue."

"Ah, William," the mayor smiled, "Surely you don't love Mississippi so much you'd want to stay here forever?"

"Not forever, just long enough. My dream is eventually to go to West Point to teach strategy."

"If Tilden wins, you'll have your transfer," Johnson said.

Mayor Johnson changed the subject.

"I saw your boy Jamie playing ball in the town diamond, just a pick-up game. He batted once while I was watching and he made a nice hit. Got thrown out trying to stretch a double into a triple, though."

"You mean to say that we Yankees are trying for too much, I suppose."

"Why, William," the mayor said cutely, "it never occurred to me that there was a parallel here. But now that you mention it – why not leave well enough alone? Why not leave the South alone?"

"Fraudulent Hayes" made a deal. Tilden conceded the election in exchange for the end of Reconstruction.

"But William, what was his alternative?" my mother said repeatedly. "If Governor Tilden had been declared winner –"

"IF! –" my father sputtered.

"– Reconstruction would have been terminated anyway," mother continued, "but in the bargain we'd have a Democrat as president."

This point always made my father fall into morose reflections. But eventually his spirit revived.

"You know, Grace, we might be able to get to West Point now. Jamie's arriving near the age when he should prep for Columbia."

I liked my life in Jefferson. My friends and I roamed all over the territory. We played baseball and fished and camped out all night in the big woods. I hunted with a double-barreled shotgun my father gave me. I had a smart red coon dog. School was easy. Returning to the North seemed like a door closing on a happy life.

Reconstruction was sure to end, but there we were, still administrating the federal agency as if it would endure for eternity.

Near the end of November Captain William Bainbridge stood at the edge of a field, holding the reins of his horse slackly in his right hand, and watching a game of baseball being played by ten to twelve year olds. Jamie was playing second base.

"The boys have solved a problem we can't manage," a voice said from behind the captain's shoulder.

"Yes, Mr. Mayor," the captain answered without turning around. "How to find time to play a ball game."

"I guess it's now too cold in New York or New Haven for baseball. Probably Princeton and Rutgers are getting ready for their eighth annual football contest. But that's a game that will never rival baseball."

"Surely not," William agreed.

A ground ball took two hops to the second baseman. Jamie played the bounce waist high and easily tossed the runner out.

"In Mississippi, though, it's still warm enough for baseball," the mayor reflected.

Johnson spoke again.

"When I said that the boys had learned to resolve conflicts that we grownups hadn't, I meant, there's your boy playing with my boy on the same team just as if there were no North or South, just ball players. But we're still at odds, my city and your federal government."

A pause.

"Well, then," Johnson continued, "Why don't we also play a game of baseball to settle our differences?"

"The Feds against the Nullifiers" – this was a jab at Johnson's idol Calhoun – "play a ball game?" my father said.

"Precisely."

"Between players from my Federal troops and your town? The war all over again between North and South?"

"But no one dies, no wives and mothers mourn, no devastation occurs, no Sherman, no Grant, no Vicksburg."

"No Stonewall Jackson, no second Bull Run."

"Just a game," Johnson said.

"Why not, indeed?"

"Done! One week from today? Right on this field?"

"Agreed."

Johnson had grown up among horsetraders and had a wager in mind.

"Bainbridge," he said, "let's make it interesting. The telegraph operator down at the station tells me that while Washington wired that

71

you must dismantle your operation before the inauguration in March, it's entirely at your discretion to wrap it up any time sooner.

"I always suspected that you intercepted our dispatches."

"Hayes will certainly honor the bargain."

My father said too sternly, "Yes, he was a Union officer. Besides, maybe it's time for the Southern states to enforce the Constitution themselves and protect the rights of the Negroes."

"The South will certainly take care of its own," Johnson said calmly. "I propose that we play baseball, and if we win you'll plan an expedient departure."

"And if *we* win? –"

"Dear fellow, the north has everything already. All we have is our tragedy, and I can't give you that. But Sally and I and the boys can give you and Grace and Jamie the best god durned unbeatable Southern fried chicken dinner with all the fixins that was ever cooked up in the history of the world. How about it?"

"I'm probably winning either way," my father said.

Jamie was batting. The two men watched. On the third pitch he lofted a foul ball in back of home plate and the catcher put it away easily.

"It's an omen," Robert said. "We will beat you badly."

I saw it all. Every man and boy in Yoknapatawpha County was there. Colonel Sutpen rode in from his hundred acres. People came from as far away as Jackson. The students from Ole Miss attended in force. Women sat in carriages a little distance away from the field. Newspaper editors came from Ripley and every other small town that had a printing press.

We boys lost use of our baseball field that whole week. Every day, Bob Johnson held tryouts, selected players, and insisted on practices. Several players showed up whom I had never before seen in Jefferson. None of my pals recognized any of them either. Jeb Rollins said that his Dad told his Mom that one player, a really big guy who said his name was "just Moose," had come all the way from Memphis to take part in the great game. Men walked around the edges of the field, hooking their thumbs into their vests, rocking back on their heels and saying things like, "The South SHALL rise again!" and "If only old Bob Lee could be here to see this." It was rumored that at least one prominent southerner had declared his intention to view the contest and cheer on the expected Southern victory. Some said that this person was Colonel Falkner, the distinguished author of *The White Rose of Memphis*, come over from Ripley. Some said the personage would be Jeb Stuart himself.

My dad and the mayor had settled upon three o'clock for the start of the game. By noon the Rebs were out on the field practicing, taking everything very seriously.

A sheriff went through the crowd requiring every man and boy to turn over Bowie knives, pistols, brass knuckles, and long guns. Ladies who merely carried two-shot derringers in their purses were, of course, courteously allowed to keep them.

At ten to three, someone shouted, "Well, we won the match by forfeit, didn't we? There's no Yankee team going to show up. Haven't got the guts, I guess." A chorus of agreement rose, and I blushed a little because I was the only Yank there and the crowd was pretty vocal about their opinion of northern manhood.

Then, at four minutes to three, a boy who had climbed up the tallest tree nearby cried out in a squeaky voice that cracked with excitement: "Here they come. Oh, lordy, I never seed such a sight!"

Nor had anyone else in Jefferson.

At precisely three o'clock, my Dad led the team onto the field. They marched in smart military order to a drum and fife and halted briskly at my Dad's order. Then they assumed parade rest positions, all in unison, like a crack drill team. I had never seen a single one of these soldiers before. Behind them marched my dad's regular troops. Dad's Jefferson team didn't have uniforms of any sort. But the team that arrived had beautiful uniforms and matching caps. On the front of their shirts, "Yankees" was inscribed.

The crowd was absolutely still and silent, except for the little boy who had been up in the tree. He was running up to astonished spectators saying, "Gully. Look at 'em. I seen 'em first, didn't I? Isn't it amazing?"

The mayor was the first to speak.

"Captain Bainbridge, it is three o'clock on the appointed day. Where sir, is your Union team?"

"You see them before you. We are ready to begin. I have the lineup in my pocket."

"Begin?"

"As agreed. I assume that since you are the home team, we will bat first. Your men can take the field, while we still have the light."

"But you have no team," Johnson said stubbornly.

"You see them before you," the captain said, waving at his men.

"I see – I see – I see," Johnson repeated as he attempted to raise himself to his maximum height, "I see a collection of Negroes wearing white uniforms. I see no team."

"You have described my team exactly," Bainbridge said. "I have with me twenty players from a Brooklyn regiment who have agreed on short notice to play your Jefferson team."

"But we can't play baseball with coloreds," Johnson said, flushed and frustrated. "You and I agreed that baseball is an American sport. These players have no part in it."

"The Constitution asserts that these players are Americans, and Americans you will accept them to be today. Or else you will forfeit the game, and you may be sure that my job will be to enforce the aims of Reconstruction rigorously to the very day of the inauguration, and especially to see to it that your recently elected Negro sheriff, Joshua Culpepper, assumes his elected office with all of its privileges."

"I didn't come from Memphis to play against *them*," Moose was heard saying to a knot of players. "I spec I'll jess go on home." Several players mumbled in agreement.

There were two umpires – Johnson's assistant Lester Donald and Lieutenant Delahanty on my dad's staff. Donald ruled on the infield and Delahanty on the outfield.

My Dad carried his lineup card over to Deputy Mayor Lester Donald, handed it to him, and said: "Sir, our lead off hitter is now going to walk to home plate with a bat in his hands. I ask you to call for the home team to take the field and to announce the name of the first batter."

Lester stared at the lineup in his hand is if he had carelessly reached out for a copperhead. He looked like a man who had been bitten and was doomed.

He was blank with astonishment. "But Cap'n, I can't call out this lineup."

"I presume that as deputy mayor you know how to read," my Dad said blandly.

"I can read surely," he said, "but not these names. These be presidents, not Negroes."

"Let me see that," the mayor demanded. He seized the lineup from Lester's hand.

He read aloud:

"First batter. George Washington, centerfield. Next, John Adams. Then, Thomas Jefferson. Batting fourth, James Madison. James

Monroe. John Quincy Adams. Andrew Jackson. Martin Van Buren. William Harrison."

"A good team roster," my Dad said. "Some revered southern names, some northern. I'm sure you can accept these names, unless the names of the presidents of the United States offend you."

It was a calculated challenge.

The most annoying kid in my class, that kind of smart aleck who answered all the questions, was standing next to me. He whispered to me, "Sure, and then come Tyler and Polk and Taylor and Pierce and –."

It was a great moment for me. "You left out Millard Fillmore," I said. He looked at me dumbly.

Everyone else but this dummy understood that my Dad was forcing the men of Jefferson to "play ball" with the Negroes. If they wouldn't, the Southerner's would lose, and they wanted to win badly.

My Dad forced the issue. He turned to the silent crowd and in the big voice that he used to call out orders at drill, he said, "Well, it seems as if there aren't any baseball players in all of Mississippi," he said in his loud company-come-to-order voice.

Some of the Old Miss students started to hiss at that.

But Mayor Johnson said, fast as could be, "We'll have none of that. We are here to play a game. And to win it." He pushed the lineup back into Lester's still outstretched hand and with forced deliberation said: "Begin the game."

"Play ball," Lester tried to shout out. But his voice was tinny and shrill.

Several players stared at Moose.

He seemed to consider the case, then announced, as he ran out to the field: "Shore, we'll kick their – ."

A shout went up even before he finished, and nine players took up their positions. John Delahanty took his position behind second base.

"First batter for the Yankees, George Washington," Lester announced.

The crowd suddenly found its voice, but it was not one voice. Some spectators booed the batter, others cheered the Rebels on, but most just shouted to let off built-up steam.

Paul Tibbets, the only one of the University Greys to survive the war, pitched for the Rebels. He wound up and threw a fastball directly at the head of George Washington. I thought to myself, here it is – he's going to bean the first batter. He wants to kill him. There's going to be a riot.

75

But the batter coolly arched his back and turned his head a hair and the ball whizzed by, past the catcher, past the umpire, and was lost in the crowd.

"Strike one," Lester Donald said.

Washington looked at the umpire with a wide grin.

"Sure fooled me," he said with a beautiful Brooklyn accent. "I calculated that it was a mite inside."

Tibbets threw his second pitch. A foot wide of the plate.

"Strike two."

"Sir," Washington said graciously, "I do thank you for indicating to me the dimensions of the strike zone. It's a tad smaller in Brooklyn."

Lester Donald jerked his thumb in the air. "That's it! Sassing the ump. You're out of here."

My dad and his Yankees rushed out to surround the umpire.

Donald crossed his arms and retreated into the umpire's classic meditative position. All protests broke upon his placid front. Washington faded into the crowd of his teammates.

"John Tyler" batting for George Washington," my Dad called. There was one strike left.

Tibbets certainly varied his pitches. His third throw hit the dirt almost ten feet from home and took a beautiful bounce straight across home plate.

"Strike three," Lester called – but prematurely, since Tyler took the ball rising on a bounce and lifted a long fly over the cernterfielder's head.

"Foul ball," Donald started to yell. But Lieutenant Delahanty was running to the outfield shouting "Fair ball." John Tyler was tearing around the bases. He reached third and stopped.

Johnson, the catcher, and the third baseman conferred at the pitcher's mound. They made no protest at Delahanty's call, though the crowd groaned.

John Adams came to bat. Tibbets wound up. The third baseman dashed over to the third base bag and knocked John Tyler off it by five feet, while Tibbets shot the ball to third to tag the runner.

"Out!" Lester Donald said.

John Tyler waved his teammates back. "Guess you picked me off fair and square," he said. "Nice of you to show me how the game's played here in the South. Sumwhat different rules than we's got in Brooklyn." He trotted over to join the other players.

John Adams jumped over home plate to reach the next pitch and hit it to the opposite field for a single. Thomas Jefferson hit a rope right over third base, a sure hit. John Adams took off. To everyone's surprise, Moose, playing third, turned out to be very agile for a big guy. He dove over the base and speared the ball, then scrambled up and threw a strike to first base.

"Double play," Lester Donald shouted. The crowd cheered.

William Henry Harrison pitched for the Yankees, with Martin Van Buren catching. They wasted no time. Harrison had a beautiful fluid motion. He poured six straight fast balls down the middle of the plate. At the end of each strikeout he made little clucking sounds of contempt for the batters. Moose, who was batting cleanup, glowered at Harrison. The third batter was Mr. Milligan, my teacher. I was sort of hoping that he could get a hit. But he never even got the bat off his shoulder. Harrison clucked. Moose glowered. As he walked to the sidelines, Harrison bowed and tipped his hat to Moose.

In the top of the second inning James Madison hit a single. James Monroe wasn't fast enough to lean back from Tibbets's pitch and had his left wrist broken. He walked off the field after touching first base and James Polk came in to run for him. John Quincy Adams singled to left and it looked like the Yankees would get James Madison home, but as soon as the ball was hit the infielders ran to home plate, and surrounded it, so that Madison couldn't touch it for a score. James Polk rounded third and headed for home too. They were both tagged out trying to get to the plate.

"That retires the side," Lester said.

"But it's only two out," my dad pointed out.

"I'm calling that Quincy feller out for illegal base running," Donald asserted.

William Henry Harrison underestimated Moose, who was first up at the end of the second. He pitched the same straight fast ball to him, right over the center of the plate, waist high. Moose lifted the ball far over the left fielder's head. It would have been out of the park in any modern stadium.

One to nothing.

For his next two times at bat, Moose saw no more fat fastballs from William Henry.

So the game went. The Rebs went down in order on strikeouts. The Yankees were kept from scoring. The trouble was, they were losing players from injuries at an alarming rate. Additional players in Yankee uniforms showed up, and by the seventh inning, the Yankees had to dip down into Vice Presidents and even cabinet officers in order to field a team. Alexander Hamilton was in centerfield. Aaron Burr was playing shortstop.

By the end of the seventh, the Yankees took a different strategy than the one they had been pursuing.

William Henry addressed the number two batter.

"Lookee here," he said, "I'm going to 'low you to hit. Get some running exercise, why don't you?"

He lobbed the ball underhand to him the way little girls throw a softball. The ball was hit slowly toward the pitcher's box. William Henry looked at it with disdain as if it were a rat in a tenement basement. The ball dribbled to his feet. He picked it up and looked grandly at the runner on first. "Nice hit," William Henry said.

The same performance was repeated with batter number three. Moose came up with two men on base.

William Henry's first pitch slammed into the dirt an inch from Moose's toes. The second ball threw up dust just beyond Moose's heels.

"Why Moose," William Henry cooed, "I believe that you do like low pitched balls."

"You better shut up," Moose said.

"Don't like low ones, then? I was mistaken," the pitcher teased him.

The third pitch just missed nicking the button on Moose's cap as he ducked for cover.

The fourth pitch steamed in. Moose couldn't move forward enough or back enough, jump up enough, or duck down enough to avoid it. It shot right at his belt buckle and doubled him up.

"Why, I do believe that that one must have slipped out of my hand," William Henry lamented coolly.

Before he finished, the Reb players, Mayor Johnson, and a considerable part of the crowd stampeded toward William Henry. A general melee broke out. Punching, gouging, poking, pummeling, and takedowns were all freely employed by both sides.

When the brawl finally broke up from exhaustion, sixteen men and one woman were carried off the field. John Tyler, Alexander Hamilton, and John Jay were sidelined for the duration.

To add insult to injury, Martin Van Buren, the Yankee catcher, had held the ball the whole time, using it to mash out assorted teeth during the fight. At the end, since no one had called time, he walked up to the runners who had been on first and second and tapped each on the shoulders with the ball as if he were knighting them. Since they were now off-base, they were out. He strode over to Moose who was still dazed, and held the ball in front of his eyes, Moose stared at it as the catcher rotated it in front of him, and then finally, nice as you please, he grazed Moose's nose with it.

"Mr. Moose," he said lowly, "I believe you're out."

"Three outs. Side retired!" Delahanty called out, while Lester Donald was struggling to get to his feet after being pinned down by two big Yankees.

Several replacements chosen from the spectators had to come in for Mississippi. In the confusion of picking out people from the crowd, one of the Reb players looked at me. I was standing there holding my glove. "You, kid," he said, "I seen you play here before. Get out in left field. No one's going to hit sheet anyhow." And I did as he said, secretly hoping I might come up to the plate and whup a fastball from William Henry.

The southerners were cautious now. With a one run lead and only two innings to hold on, they adopted the safest strategy possible. Tibbets went through the motions of pitching without delivering a ball.

The days get short in early December in Mississippi. Night was falling fast. Seen from home plate the outfielders were already only dim figures.

Aaron Burr came up to bat in the top of the eighth. Tibbets went into his windup. His arm swung down. The catcher pounded his mitt.

"Strike one," Lester Donald announced.

"I don't recerlect a ball passing by me," Aaron complained.

The catcher held his glove up for Burr and Donald to see. A ball was in it.

Tibbets went through his pitching motion again.

"Strike!" Lester called.

"I thought it a bit outside," Aaron Burr mentioned.

"I said, 'STRIKE!'" Lester insisted. "Now I say, 'Three Strikes!'" Tibbets had not even gone through his pitching motions this time. Likewise, John Adams and John C. Calhoun were called out on three straight strikes each from the invisible ball.

William Henry resumed his old style of pitching and the Yankees were soon at bat again for the ninth inning. I hadn't had a chance at the plate.

Henry Clay went down on strikes, though this time the batter went through the motions of swinging at a ball that wasn't there. Tibbets wondered if the Yankees had really been fooled. But after taking one strike Millard Fillmore clutched his side, cried out in pain, opened his

79

hand, and a ball dropped to the ground. "Hit batter," Delahanty called out. "Take first!"

Lester had no time to object. One out. One man on. Andrew Jackson, "Old Hickory," came to the plate. Tibbets went elaborately through his motions.

One strike. A second.

Darkness was nearly total. Only the full moon illuminated the field.

Tibbets wound up and hurled air. Andy gave a mighty swing. The crack of a bat sounded sharply. Or was it the sound of a small mortar being fired from the woods? In any event, the spectators and players saw a pristine white ball trailing streaks of glory, ascending into the heavens and passing across the moon. Where it landed wasn't known until two days later when a boy retrieved it from the riverbank a quarter mile away.

Preceded by Millard Fillmore, the hero of the Battle of New Orleans trotted majestically around the bases. Tibbets ran up to Lester saying, "But I didn't pitch anything." But Mayor Johnson came out and said, "Bill, just let it go. Southern honor should be tested no more today."

Two runs to one. Feds ahead.

I did come up to bat in the bottom of the ninth. Whether William Henry threw me a ball or not I never could be sure. I could hardly see my hands when I stretched my arms out. I did swing the third time he delivered, and missed. William Henry whistled and said: "Powerful swing, white boy. Sure glad you didn't connect."

The game was over.

A line of wagons emerged from the woods as the last pitch was thrown, and the players hustled into them and were gone before anyone could think about lynching and such like.

The crowd drifted away. It was past time for dinner, and now food to be eaten assumed more importance than a game that had been lost. Life went on. Moose passed by, talking to a friend about greens and end pieces of bacon with grits.

I walked over and stood between my dad and mom.

"So you're a left fielder," my Dad said, with his hand on my shoulder.

"Second base," I answered. "They played me out of my position."

We stood there waiting until only one other man remained at the field.

Bob Johnson came over and put out his hand.

"William," he said, "that was a game. I 'spec we'll have you for months now you've won the wager?"

"Actually, I decided to close up and move out end of next week. We'll be in New York for Christmas. I'm surprised that the telegrapher down at the railroad station didn't pick up the message and inform you."

"Don't know as he didn't," Johnson answered. "Anyway, the missus has been home for the last three innings, preparing dinner. The South's been properly reconstructed now. Let's eat."

THE BOTTLE-BAT

Hank met Anna in Cincinnati through "Permanent Partners." After a half hour, he was completely bored and about to bolt from Otto's Coffee Shop even before Anna had entirely forked her way through an enormous serving of Black Forest cake.

Then she mentioned Heine Groth.

"Ja," she said, "I've always dreamed of meeting a baseball player. Every since I was a girl my father would talk to anyone who would listen about our ancestor Heine Groth, the great hitter."

"Heine Groth?" he wondered.

The name rang distant bells in his memory. Wasn't he one of the old-time players written about in *They Played the Game*, a book he had read as a child? Someone around the time of Wee Willie Keeler, Cap Anson, and Eddie Collins?

"Heine Groth and his bottle-bat. Whenever my father had the chance, he would bring it out. "Mein father owned a bar downtown, 'Heine's Hofbrau Haus.' He had the idea that here in Cincinnati he could build up a big clientele through his family association with Heine Groth. Of course, most of his customers had no idea who Heine Groth was. But that was an extra incentive for my father.

'What!' he'd say, 'You don't remember who Heine Groth vas? Heine Groth and his bottle-bat. Does that jog your memory? *Ja*, he vas the player who saw that bats were designed all wrong. They tapered, like burgundy bottles. You had only about six inches to get good wood on the ball. Heine made the perfect bat, shaped like a bottle, with a slim rod for a handle, topped by a solid column of gut vood straight as a bottle of claret wine.'

"At this moment, my father would bring up an empty wine bottle that he kept below the bar especially for these occasions.

"'Do you see,' he'd ask, 'the smarts of his idea? Anywhere on this column that the bat struck the ball would be the same. The bottle-bat.'

"'But vait,' he'd add, 'I have the bat itself. Where did I put it?'

"He'd say this because he decided it would increase the suspense for the customers if it seemed doubtful that the bat would be found, and this would enlarge the drinker's pleasure when the authentic treasure was retrieved. After a minute or so my father would produce the bottle-bat. He'd carefully wipe away any puddles of beer that might still remain on the bar, then lay the bat down, smiling, as if the two of them had entered into a secret society whose sign was the bottle-bat.

82

"The pinnacle of success for my father would come when the customer was so intrigued that he might say, shyly, something like, 'Could I touch it?' or 'Maybe I could give it a swing?' Then, like a grandmaster of the Knights Templar who had just produced a chunk of the True Cross, my father would wrinkle his brow in concern, but graciously say, 'Why yes, if you are careful. You can see its value.'

"One swing, possibly two would be allowed, and then my father would whisper, 'We don't want to wear it out, do we?' and he'd put it back in its place. 'But,' he'd add, 'Come back often, come back, and I'll bring it out again. *Ja,* come and bring your friends, and you yourself can give them a special treat by telling them the story of Heine Groth's bottle-bat, just as I've told it to you.'

"It didn't work. Few customers showed any interest in Heine Groth. Most times, before my father could bring out the bat, customers would say things like, 'Don't you have any pretzels in this place?' or, 'Say, would you change the channel?' Then my father would sulk. Soon he formed a violent grudge in advance against all customers, regarding them as boors who did not deserve even to hear the story, much less glimpse the sacred wood. Heine's Hofhrau Haus lasted a year."

"And your father?" Hank asked.

"Dead. He died of a broken heart."

"And the bat? Was it really one that actually belonged to Heine Groth?"

"I have it. It's somewhere around the house."

Anna had a point of interest after all.

"I'd really like to see that bat," he said.

"Sure," she replied casually. "Next time the Phillies comes back here, call me, come over and take a look at it."

"Say, we're here for a three-game series, how's about I come over tomorrow morning? What's your address?"

Anna agreed to make search for the bat, gave him her address and directions, and they set a time.

In high school Hank Wagner was a star. Now he was a utility infielder. If a left-hander was throwing he'd sometimes pinch hit in late innings, but with a career batting average of .237 he was frequently traded. In seven seasons, he had been on the rosters of three teams.

He arrived promptly at Anna's house. "I haven't found the bat yet," she said, "but sit down at the table here. I've made a nice apple strudel.

83

There's coffee on the stove and cream in the icebox. Eat. Look at the scrapbook if you want."

The strudel was really delicious. The coffee simmered in a big blue porcelain pot with egg shells floating in it.

Many of the old photos in the scrapbook were of Heine Groth wearing an old-fashioned baseball outfit with a flat-top cap, posing with the famous bottle-bat cocked over his shoulder. In a few he held a flimsy fielder's glove at the ready. Besides these, were charming old photos of picnics and outings where whiskered men in straw bowlers were hoisting mountainous schooners of beer and stuffing themselves with sausages. Hank's own great grandparents come from Germany, but he knew nothing else about them. Anna came in carrying the bat, the wonderful bottle-bat, in her upraised arms as if it were an offering.

"Here it is," she said. "Dad said Heine called it 'Thor's hammer.'"

"It's a real Kaiser-weapon," Hank said.

She looked surprised and amused. "Dad called it that, too," she said.

"It's very dark wood," he said, taking it into his hands. "but light in weight."

"I'm told it's ash. Dad said that Heine Groth treated it with tobacco juice – 'to give it strength,' he said. That's how ash got this dark color, I guess."

"Do you mind?" he asked, as he got up from the chair and moved to an open space in the room.

"No, go ahead and give it a swing. It'd be something to have a real baseball player swing it again."

He swung. "Over the fence," Anna cried out gleefully. "An *echt* homer." She clapped her hands.

The bat felt good in his hands. His own fingers slid perfectly into the invisible grooves made long ago by the hands of Heine Groth. He swung again.

"I wish I could hit something with it," he said wistfully.

"Let's go to the park," she said. "We can walk. It's two blocks away. I'll pitch to you. I saw a box of old baseballs with my Dad's stuff."

They proved to be ancient balls, scuffed and grass-stained. Some were stitched very differently from modern balls.

"Just wait a minute before we go," she said, "and I'll make some roast beef sandwiches. We can have a picnic."

At the park was a big square field with a backstop and diamond in each corner. They went to one of the fields and ran the bases a few times to warm up. Anna was in good shape. Anna went about ten feet in front of the mound and got ready to pitch. He settled in at home plate.

"I'm worried about breaking the bat," he said. "It's a piece of baseball history. I wouldn't want to ruin it."

"Don't worry," she said, "there's a bottle-bat in the Cooperstown Hall of Fame, right next to a big photo of great grand dad. This one is not the only one in existence, after all."

"Still, it has to be valuable to a collector."

"Well, I think it will be all right. Dad says that this bat was used through several seasons, and it's still in one piece. You said you wanted to hit."

At that she sent a ball his way, just outside the plate. He was surprised. The bat came around awkwardly and the ball skidded foul off its top. He swung the bat a few times more to get its feel. Then he felt the groove. It was not his usual swing, but one that the bat demanded.

"O.K. Now pitch," he called. Anna's slow pitch came in over the middle of the plate. The bat swung and the ball shot down, hitting about thirty feet from home. It took a big high bounce over Anna's head and didn't come down until it passed over second base. A single in any baseball park.

He held the bat loosely and let it swing itself, take its own arc. It swung the same way every time, so that where the ball landed depended on where it had been thrown. If low to middle height, the ball was beaten into the ground. If up above the belt, the ball leaped into the air. It never traveled very far. The grounders bounced before the baselines, then over the heads of where infielders would stand. Balls hit into the air were easy line drives landing between the infield and outfield. Balls pitched outside to him, a right-handed batter, went to right field. Inside pitches went to left. Holding the bat with his pinky finger curled over the knob or choking up four inches produced different hits. You could do anything with this bat. It was a magic bat with a will of its own.

"Let's eat," Anna said merrily when she had thrown through her whole stock of balls five times. "I'm starved."

She laid out her picnic. Roast beef sandwiches were followed by pickles, green cherry tomatoes, sauerkraut, potato salad with onions, peppers in oil and vinegar, and stewed apples with cinnamon.

"This will put some meat on your bones for your game tonight," she told him.

"I guess I will have plenty of meat on my bones tonight. That was an authentic Heine Groth meal," he said. "How did those old guys do it?

85

Lucky I'm probably not playing tonight. I don't get a lot of playing time. I suppose you know that. If I had to run bases, I'd be weighed down by this big feed."

"Maybe you'd have more energy," she interjected.

"I don't want to sound ungrateful," he said. "I'm glad I had it. I'm glad we had a picnic together. I've really enjoyed it all."

At the house she had a whole closet of momentos from the early days of baseball, passed down from Heine to his first born son, then to his son, and finally to Anna. She even had the battered flat-top cap and the flimsy glove.

"I've meant to send them to Cooperstown," she said, "but I suppose I must have saved them for someone just like you, someone who would appreciate them."

"I really like these old things. Maybe I should have been one of those early players," he said.

Anna stood there with her hands on her hips, beaming, as he spoke. When he finished, she stepped up to him pertly, put his face between her hands and planted a big hearty kiss on his lips.

"That's for dessert," she said.

"How's about a second helping?" he joked.

"Sure," she said, and did it all over again.

When he left, she pulled the side pocket of his slacks open and shoved in a handful of hard candies from Munich.

"Give you something to suck on while you're sitting on the bench," she smiled.

He did sit the game out on the bench, just as he predicted.

Two days after they left Cincinnati, Johnny Post, the regular shortstop, tore up his right leg sliding into home and was washed up for the season. Hank had to sub at short. Post had been hitting .297 and batting second. Hank had been at the plate only 87 times all year and was now batting .218, low man on the team. Some of the pitchers had higher averages.

Five games later, when his average fell to .185, Jake Diamond, his skipper, called him in for a little chat.

"Hank," he started, "it looks like you're not doing much for the team. We've got a shortstop who's done pretty well in the minors, and I'm thinking of bringing him up and sending you down. Maybe you're just in a slump. I'll play you through the Cincinnati games, but you've got to make some showing.

86

"I know, Jake. Thanks for giving me a chance. I've got a good feeling about Cincinnati."

But he didn't really have a good feeling. That's when he thought of calling Anna again.

"I know it's late," he said, "but would you mind if I came over tomorrow morning to see you?"

"I'd be glad to see you," she said. "Come for breakfast if you wish. I get up early."

"Nine."

"Eight if you want."

He rang the bell exactly at eight.

There were potato pancakes with sour cream, flaky pastries shaped like pretzels and filled with apricot preserve, sizzling sausages bursting their skins, sour rye rolls with fennel, orange flavored chocolate sticks, a bowl of egg salad, fatty goose livers, big slices of Black Forest and Westphalia ham, a dish of beets sweetened with honey, and an uncorked bottle of caraway schnapps.

"There you are," she said. "Choose what you like." She did a good mail order business in sending homemade meals to homesick Germans in America.

"The team's doing ok," he said, "Us and the Reds could face off in the playoffs. We're in the running for the wild card. The Reds are sure to be in the playoffs."

"That would be thrilling," Anna responded cheerily.

"But I'm not doing so well myself." His tone turned serious now. "In fact, I'm just about to get canned. Those kisses you gave me for luck didn't work."

"I didn't give you kisses for luck," she said. "They were for dessert. If you wanted a kiss for luck, you should have asked."

"I wish I had. I really needed a lucky kind of kiss."

She didn't offer to give him one though.

He hemmed and hawed for a while, then he came out with what he really wanted.

"Anna, do you remember when you pitched to me in the park and I was using the Heine Groth bottle-bat? It felt just right. Maybe I'm a reincarnation of good old Heine. It was right for him, and it was right for me. It's just my kind of bat. I checked out the regulation book for bats and it still would pass under the current rules. I talked to a furniture maker about creating one. But it just wouldn't be the same – it wouldn't have that nice black, magic stain squirted from Heine's own mouth."

"I guess it's a bat that's seen a lot of hits," she returned.

"And it's probably got a lot more stored up in it. I'd bet it does."

They were both silent for a minute.

"That's why I was wondering," he said, "if I could borrow the bat. Maybe some of the hits Heine Groth didn't use up will be waiting in it for me."

She didn't hesitate a bit.

"Why not? Give it a try. You slammed the ball at the park pretty well. Of course, the Cincinnati pitchers are not going to dish up meatballs for you the way I did."

"I've got a good feeling about it though," he said. "Maybe it'll just give me the edge I need. I'll try not to break it."

"Oh," Anna said, "I heard on the radio that there was a Stradivarius that got all smashed up, almost to splinters, and it got put back good as new. Don't worry. It's just a bat."

She went to the broom closet in the kitchen and retrieved the bat. It looked blacker and denser.

"It's a Thor's hammer," he said. He liked the way Anna had said that.

"You know, my mother said that her grandmother, Heine Groth's wife, always said that the bat was only part of Heine's success. 'The rest vas the kuchen I made him. Days I gave him good *kuchen*, he hit. Days I gave him nothing, he was *kaput*'."

Before he left, Anna opened the refrigerator and took out a package wrapped in aluminum foil.

"I made you a meat loaf sandwich for later, with Düsseldorf mustard," she said, patting him on the tummy.

The bottle-bat did its magic. That same night Hank went five for five. His average soared twenty-two points in one game.

The Phillies swept the series. Hank's average rose to an astronomical .236. Everyone noticed that with this funny bat he had changed his batting style. He sent high bouncing balls into the turf and by the time they returned to earth he had nearly reached first. He dropped soft fly balls just out of reach of the infielders. No matter how they tried to play him, the bat found a hole somewhere. When the outfielders played close in to grab his short flies, he slid his hands down on the bat to its very end and ripped drives just over their heads. He kept on hitting game after game.

88

One of the old sportswriters saw it. "In a game that has come to be dominated by power," he wrote, "we haven't seen hitting of the kind Hank Wagner is doing since Wee Willie Keeler, unless it's Nellie Fox. He's turning into an old-fashioned artist with the stick."

Nine games later, with fifty-six hits in a hundred and eighty-four at bats, his average had risen to .306. Jake took him from the eighth spot and put him in lead off. During this twelve game stretch in September, no one in the league had a higher average.

"I guess all you needed was a good talking to from me," Jake Diamond told Hank one day. "You started hitting just after I threatened to bounce you down to the minors."

"That was it, Jake. You just had to knock me off my duff."

"Tough love – it works," Jake said.

"You got it, Jake."

"Keep it up, Hank. The team's leaning on you. You're sort of carrying us now."

It was true. Like being back in his high school days – he was a star again. He even stole a base and kept stealing them.

By the last game of the season, Hank's average had climbed to .317. Of course, he didn't have enough at bats to qualify for the official list of .300 hitters but the press liked his Cinderella story.

Anna put up her best meals in dry ice and shipped them to him.

Although they had an inferior record to Cincinnati's, the Phillies went into the playoffs as the favorites. "Momentum" is what the sportswriters said they had. "Anyone who has a Hank Wagner baseball card, better hold onto it," one writer quipped.

The day before the playoffs were scheduled to begin he spent the day with Anna.

They talked. They had a catch. They hit pepper to each other with Heine's bat. The day ended with a big juicy beefsteak seared and then roasted in a burgundy reduction and smothered in onions, served with mounds of home fries and asparagus thicker than a man's thumb.

Eventually he said, "Anna, I'd better go. It's a big game tomorrow, the start of the playoffs."

"Good luck," she answered warmly.

"Why don't you give me that good luck kiss now, then? I'm asking."

"Kiss you for luck? Of course, I will."

She didn't wait for him, but stepped right up and locked her hands in back of his head, pulling his face down to hers.

"How was that?" she asked.

"Perfect," he said truthfully.

"All right, then. Good luck."

He started out the door, then turned, smiling.

"Where did you put my Kaiser hammer?" he asked. "With a kiss like that, I came near to forgetting it."

"I didn't," she said.

He knew at once. They had left it in the park.

They searched, of course. But it was gone.

"But I need it for the game," he whined.

"Hank, you can hit with any bat. You could get hits with a tree branch. You could borrow a broomstick from the kids in the street and hit just as well with that. It's not the bat, not the bottle-bat, Hank. *You* are Thor's hammer, if you only knew it and could believe in it. It's not the cooking either. Mama Groth was wrong."

"I need the bat," he sulked.

He was feeling really sour and panicked now.

"My life is ruined," he moaned.

He was so frustrated he wanted to throw himself on the floor and beat his fists against it.

"Good night," she said sternly.

And pushed him out the door.

He had been horrible. He had acted like a baby. He knew that. And he hadn't even gotten a luscious piece of Anna's paprika chicken to take with him.

It was a best of five series. In the first game Hank used a deep black Louisville Slugger bat. But it had no mind of its own. He couldn't hit with it.

Late at night he roused out of bed a woodworker whose name he found in the yellow pages.

"Meet me at your shop. I'll tell you what to do."

The second playoff game Hank came to the batter's box with his newly manufactured bottle-bat. His grounders didn't bounce high enough. His flies were handled in easy over-the-head catches by the infielders.

After the game he said to Jake: "You'd better call up that shortstop down on the farm. I'm done for."

"Snap out of it," was all Diamond answered.

90

The next day was a travel day while the teams moved to Philadelphia for the third game. Hank did not travel with the team and he did not show up for the team meeting. He was not there for batting practice. He was nowhere to be found. Jake called the police and also put the team's detective to work.

But on the morning of the next day everyone knew where Hank was. He was in jail.

On the very front page of the papers Hank was splashed in the headlines. STAR PHILLIES SHORTSTOP ARRESTED IN COOPERSTOWN, NEW YORK. BREAKS INTO BASEBALL HALL OF FAME.

Hank confessed everything.

He told the reporters that he was nothing without a true Heine Groth bottle-bat. So he made his way to Cooperstown. He got there just before closing time and checked a package in the coatroom. He hid himself in the janitor's closet. He waited until two a.m. when he felt certain that all the security inspections for the evening had been made. Then he made his way through the dark museum. He went to the coat room where he had checked the package. From it he extracted his replica bat. He jimmied the glass case housing the real Cooperstown bat and exchanged his replica bat for it.

He started to wrap up the real bat. His plan was to place this in the coat room, then in the morning, when the museum opened up, to leave his hiding place in the closet, retrieve his package and exit, getting back to Philadelphia with his treasure by night for the third game.

He might have brought all this off successfully, too. But as he told the interrogators, he made one mistake.

"I was so thrilled to have a real Heine Groth bat back in my hands again that I thought, just before I wrap it up I'll take one good swing. I did. It felt great. I was batting against Iron Joe McGinty, that's what I was pretending. In the dark I didn't notice anything in back of me. So on my follow through I smashed a case containing a beaten-up glove and uniform used by Wee Willie Keeler. Bells went off. Lights snapped on. Security guards rushed to me. I stood there like the centerfield flagpole, dumb as a post. The bat was wrenched from my hands. I was slammed to the ground. You know the rest. Handcuffs. Questions about terrorism. Phone calls to Homeland Security."

"And you were actually going to use the bat in tonight's game?"

"Sure. It's my bat, it was made for me. I'm a reincarnation of Heine Groth. Damn that Wee Willie Keeler. He always was a troublemaker."

A psychologist was called in by the local authorities. When she emerged from an hour's consultation, she told reporters, "Now boys, I can't say much. Patient-Doctor confidentiality, you know. But I'd call this a case of dissociation. Maybe a unique case of multiple personality. Sometimes he seems to think of Heine Groth as his hero. At other times, he says he is reincarnated. He talks about an Anna and dwells on the urgency in getting back to her for sauerbraten, "rotkohl," whatever that is, and späetzle, which I believe are noodles. Or dumplings. Anyway, as I told the police captain here, Mr. Wagner is not, in my opinion, criminally responsible. If he has a trial, I'll testify that this is a remarkable case of delusion."

In answer to a reporter's question, she added: "No, he does not believe he is Honus Wagner. His delusion revolves wholly around Heine Groth – and sauerbraten."

Bob Costas showed that clip on the six o'clock news. A story in the afternoon edition added a few more details. The archivist of the Hall of Fame told the FBI, "The most ironical part of this is that the bottle-bat we have on display is only a replica itself. He swapped a new replica for an old replica. Heine Groth never touched that bat. So far as we could discover in our research not a single authentic bottle-bat exists. Several years ago, a grandson of Heine Groth's sent in a bat for us to authenticate. He said he kept it in a bar to show off to customers, and he hoped we would give him a certificate. But it too proved to be a replica. A few hundred of them were produced in Louisville as souvenirs when Heine Groth was at the peak of his popularity, and they all had easily identifiable markings at the end of the knob."

A reporter pointed out that during the last month when Hank had made such a remarkable record, several papers had printed articles about Hank's use of the genuine old bottle-bat.

The archivist merely replied politely, "Well, you can't believe everything you read in the funny papers."

Hank appeared before a judge and was released on bail.

He missed game three. A substitute for him was hastily called up from the minors.

In Philadelphia, a group of diehard fans formed a "Hank Wagner Defense Club." Bill O'Reilly made him the subject of a segment on the "Most Ridiculous Item of the Day."

Innocent until officially proven guilty, he was allowed to play in the fourth game. He actually got a single in the sixth, using a bat borrowed from Johnny Post. Though there were a few boos when he first took the field, the fans rallied to the side of the accused and applauded him loudly. The twelve members of the Hank Wagner Defense Club all stood to give him an ovation. Still, the Reds won this fourth game.

Afterward, Hank asked Jake to leave him on the bench for the fifth game. He said he didn't want to be the center of attention. He didn't deserve it, he felt.

Jake said, "You know I'd stick up for you. I wouldn't let you down if you wanted to play. We've still got a chance, you know. But I see your point."

Hank watched from the dugout as the Reds took the series in five.

For him the season was ended, though he had been remanded for psychiatric treatment in Philadelphia and would have to face charges in New York. The club's attorney gave him assurances that as a baseball player, and taking into consideration his shaky, "overstrained" psychological state. Given that the item he intended to steal was worth no more than the value of the wood, and that all the damage he caused amounted only to the demolishment of one glass display case, he would probably be sentenced to a fine and community service when his case came up.

Hank went to a court-appointed psychologist. At the first session, he began to laugh uncontrollably. She was alarmed. She considered calling 911. But when the hysteria subsided he said, "The kicker is that all along I was using a phony bottle-bat. I guess I talked myself into becoming a star, when I had it in me, not in the bat, all along. I was really fucked up, wasn't I? It drove me crazy. And now I see how I fucked myself up."

"You're cured of your delusion, then," she said with relief. "But I still think you need treatment for profound insecurity. We have months until spring training to get to the bottom of this. Now, tell me about your mother."

A week later, he picked up the phone. Anna was on the other end. It was the first time she had ever called him.

"Sorry about the bat," she said.

"So it was a phony bat I borrowed from you, after all."

"I always suspected as much," she admitted, "though I wasn't sure. But it was the genuine article to you."

93

Then he said what had already been in his mind even before Anna called.

"I'm thinking of swinging through Cincinnati sometime soon. Are you going to be around?"

"Just like always. My mail order business, you know. At the end of next week I'm expecting a choice shipment of fresh wild boar loins from Bavaria, I'll slice them into tournedos filets and top them up with a morel mushroom *chausseur* sauce, finished with a glazed Syrah reduction. Of course, I'll send them out frozen, but next week I'll still have a few fresh ones around. Interested in tasting one?"

"I sure am. Name the day."

"Well," she said, "the World Series between the Reds and the Yankees is scheduled to start on Wednesday. Why don't we watch it together?"

And top off the day with a sauerbraten?"

"Sauerbraten? Sure. You could help me. I'll make you my *sous chef* this winter. Stay a while and we'll watch the team videos of how you swung the bottle-bat. You'll get your swing back. Next season you'll be cooking on both burners."

THE FOUR HUNDRED

So, it's the last day of the season, I'm batting .39937. Close to the magic .400. And tonight I've got to bat against Tony Cavazzini. He's my best friend, and Susan's too. Susan's been my wife for nearly six months. Tony and I were teammates until this season, when he was traded to the Cardinals. Don't ask me why. He's the best pitcher in the league. He's got a split finger change up.

If you are me, you're thinking, this is probably my only chance to hit .400. Nobody's done it since Ted Williams. That was so long ago who knows when it was? In the forties, maybe. But Williams was in the American League and I'm in the National. I don't know who the last guy was to do it in the National. There was a guy named George Sisler, he did it, but I don't know if he was in the National or not. What am I, a baseball historian?

And me, I never even came close before. Always .320, .317, .321, like that. A .322 was my highest. I dunno, I just have the feeling I'll never have a season like this again, not even close. And this is my twelfth season. I'm pushing thirty-five and I sure won't have many more. This year's as much a surprise to me as to anyone else.

How'd I jump up this year? I didn't take no steroids, didn't get hypnosis, change bats, wear the same mismatched socks every day to keep the luck rolling. Nothing. Same swing. Same stance.

This season, everything clicked. End of May, .317. Same old stuff, looked like a standard season for me. June, .329. End of July, .346. August, .380. On September 22, the old average slid over .400 for the first time, 4003, then it swung all around that number, one day .401, .402, the next .398 or something like that, as we go into October.

Why can't a guy just get to the last day of the season batting a big fat .425 and not worry about getting any hits at all?

Susan is hot for me to hit .400. "Gee," she says, "You'll be in the record books. You'll get a big raise, don't you think? You're my guy, and they'll all point me out and say, 'Isn't it great? – she's married to a .400 hitter'."

There's something called the Four Hundred in society. The top four hundred of the swellest elite, I guess. But .400 in baseball is a small club.

I'd sure like to do it for Susan. It's something we could remember together when I'm retired and we're sitting on a porch someday in

Sarasota or some other place where old folks go. Then we could say, "What about that year I hit .400, huh?" That'd be a swell memory.

My mother could be proud too. She's hardly ever satisfied, but she might say something like, "So, you've done something right at last, haven't you?" That's as proud as she'd let herself show. But I'd like it even if she said just that. You can laugh if you want, but that's how I feel.

Maybe I'd do it, hit .400 for the old man. He's dead now, but maybe he's with some of his old pals up in heaven, and he'll look down and say, "Hey, that's my kid. A .400 hitter. Can you believe that?"

I'd like to do it for myself. It'd be the best thing I've even done, except for marrying Susan, which was a really fantastic thing to do.

So, this is it. Today. In the mornings before games I usually lay around. Sometimes Susan lays around too and we fool around. But this morning she says she's got errands to run. She'll see me later, or she'll wave to me at the game anyway.

I'm alone. I don't feel like lying in bed. Am I nervous? I guess so, I guess I am. You'd be too.

I think, well I'll stop over and see Mom. Maybe she'll have coffee on and we'll sit down in the living room and look out the window and talk in a nice way.

She has this old place with a front porch. You walk up the steps and stand in front of the door and ring the bell. The door's got an oval glass panel with flowers etched into it. You can't see in the house from there because the glass is frosted. But that's ridiculous because if you just step over to the right and look in the living room window you can see everything that's going on inside. And when I tell you what happened you'll see I mean everything.

I get up and throw on some sweats and drive over to Mom's. I don't even have breakfast first because I sort of think, maybe Mom will have something in the house, nothing fancy, cereal and milk and maybe even a banana. I'm thinking, maybe she hasn't even eaten yet, and we'll have breakfast together.

She had a banana all right. Because when I walk up the front steps, quiet-like, thinking I won't ring the bell even, I'll just surprise her. I tip toe over to the window and what do I see but some big guy on top of Mom on the living room couch with his pants around his ankles and his shoes still on, and her with her housecoat not even unzipped, just pulled up around her armpits. And he's putting his big banana into her good.

96

O.K, so that's why a big Cadillac is parked a few doors down the street. Some breakfast he's having.

Of course, I don't tap on the glass. I step back away from the window. And then I can't help it, I just take another look and boy are they going at it, really enjoying themselves. I bet Mom will say something to him when they're done more than, "Well, you've made something of yourself at last."

I guess I won't have any time with Mom after all, but I can't resist taking one more peek. When I edge over to the window, they've changed position and she's on top and the guy is lying on his back with his eyes shut tight, but huffing and puffing and tossing all around.

My Mom, who's fifty-two but not showing it, looks around, out the window, and stares right at me. At first she doesn't see anything. I guess she's kind of focused elsewhere, so to speak. Then she does see me. Maybe at first she blushes a little or maybe she doesn't, but in a second she gets her composure, and she looks straight at me – and winks! How do you like that? Your mom is doing someone and she looks up and winks at you. What does it mean?

It doesn't mean anything. She just doesn't know what else to do. It's a strange greeting, but I sort of like it, I like her wink. She's never winked at me before. Is this a good way to start my big day? Could be.

I'm driving away, thinking about tonight's game and then I go back to remembering my Mom, and sure enough I'm not paying attention. I've never been a good driver anyway. I'm too much of a dreamer. What else? On this day I would have to rear-end a guy in a Taurus who is standing still at a stop light.

It's not a big crash. I bang my knee a little. I don't think this will be a problem tonight. I mash his bumper up and shatter his rear light. It's not much. I don't have any damage at all, just a little green smear on my bumper. I can buff that off with some rubbing compound, no problem. The driver turns out to be a nice guy though. He's dressed in a suit and all. When he exits the car and walks back, looking a little flushed, he eyes me, then smiles and says, "Why, you play for the Cubs, don't you?"

I have a little luck anyway. The guy is a Cubs fan. He says, "Wait till I tell my kid. I've been rear-ended by the batting champ. Could I have your autograph for my boy?"

He forgets all about the little plastic pieces of his red rear light lying on the street.

"I'll do better than that," I say. I'll give you an autograph, sure. But you're supposed to ask for my insurance info. And you'll get that too.

I'm really sorry. I wasn't paying attention. What I'll do," I say, "let me get you passes to tonight's game. How about that?"

"Gosh, that's ok," he says. "I'm glad to meet you."

He was a swell guy. I'll give him two passes for the game, one for himself and one for his kid. It's just the two of them. I wonder if he has a Mom too, but I don't ask.

I always carry some passes around with me. There's plenty of seats in Wrigley Field. What with the rest of the team making a .237 average and us losing ninety-seven games, not counting tonight, the interest of the fans generally drops off at the end of the season.

The guy whose Taurus I bashed says he sure will be there tonight to cheer me on, and his kid will never forget that the same guy who smashed his Dad's car ends the season with a .400 average.

Ten-thirty in the morning. Susan sits on the edge of the king-size bed in a nice hotel room far away from the one where visiting teams always stay. She walks over to the window to watch the cars whizz by. Then she goes back to the bed and sits down again. She's been sitting in the room for about a half hour, thinking of nothing.

The door is unlatched. On the handle outside swings a "Do Not Disturb" sign that she hung there.

Tony Cavazzini comes through the door and closes it behind him.

"Susan," he says, leaning back against the doorjam.

"Hi, Tony," she answers brightly.

"Long time, no see."

"Really. Good to see you."

"You too."

She motions to a chair that faces the foot of the bed.

"Sit down, why don't you? Tell me how things are going, Tony."

He takes the chair. She adds, "You've had a great season. No one deserves it more. Anyone who can win eleven games with the Cubs can post twenty or thirty wins with a team that makes the playoffs."

"I tell you, I was glad to be traded. They knew I'd be a free agent this year anyway, and I wouldn't stay a day more than I had to, so they got something in return for me."

"Miss me a little?" she asks. "Me and Larry?"

"Sure. You guys are my two best friends, aren't you?"

"Larry thinks the world of you.... Me too."

"We had good times. We sure did."

98

"Larry says maybe you'll stay over a day or two after the game. He told me to call you up at the hotel and ask you, "'Why don't you stay over a while, Tony?'"

"We're going to be having meetings and practices. But maybe I could spend tomorrow and leave on a late plane."

She changes the subject.

"So, you're pitching tonight?"

"I guess."

"Larry's going for .400."

"This is his year. A pitcher can't do much with a lousy team, but a batter is on his own. Maybe with other hitters in the lineup that aren't doing much, he won't set a record for at-bats or drive in a ton of runners, but he can always hit for an average. And it's the average, when it's a four hundred, that counts, isn't it?"

"I sure want him to make it, Tony."

"Susan," he says, sort of half-joking, "You didn't ask me to come here to bribe me to let up on Larry tonight?"

"Of course I did," she says in her joking voice. "Sure, I'd like you to give him some pitches he can hit every time he comes up. Who could tell? The way he's been swinging he's gone lots of games with two, three, four hits. He went five for five against the Brewers two weeks ago and even won that game with a triple against the best reliever in the League. You know who I mean. Who would know that your split finger didn't split, or whatever it does?

"I'd know."

"You know I'm joking. Give Larry your best pitch. This year he could go two for four against anyone in the League."

"So?" he asks.

"What I really wanted is just to see you. We never really said a proper goodbye to each other. We were close. I don't know how to say it. You're still a part of any heart. But I have to let you go. I want to be sure there's no hard feelings. This has nothing to do with Larry. It's sort of our final goodbye. But I want it to be happy"

"Susan, I remember how we were before we broke up and you started with Larry later. I remember it very well. Very well."

She isn't really listening to him now. She had planned out what she was going to do. She is intent on that.

"Yes," she says, "I do too. Do you see what I'm wearing?"

"A yellow dress. So?"

99

"No, I mean this," she says, and she stands up in front of the bed and in one motion pulls her sheath over her head and drops it in back of her on the bed.

"Don't you remember this?" she whispers. She has nothing on under her sheath, no underwear, bare legs, no jewelry, not even the diamond navel stud she got a month ago from Larry, just a gold chain cinching her waist.

"I remember how good we were together. I remember when I gave you that chain," he says. "When I put it on you. Of course I do." He looks her up and down, but in a nice appreciative way.

"Of course I remember," he says.

He comes over to her and, not pressing against her, kisses her lips gently, and she lets him.

She rests her hands on his shoulders.

"Now I want you to take it back," she says, laughing.

The sunlight plays on her creamy skin.

He circles his arms around her waist – leaning into her. He lets the chain fall like a golden shower into one palm.

"I really love Larry now," she says. "You know?"

"I know. Of course."

He sits back on the chair and watches her dress.

"I love you too," she says.

"Everything lasts," is all he says.

Neither of them understood why their goodbye should be this way, but both behaved perfectly as if they had always known how it must be.

"Now we leave?" he asks.

"Sure. See you tomorrow."

They leave separately. He goes first. She leaves the door ajar. When she hears the elevator door close, she goes out too.

"What I want you to do is this," the vice-president of the Cubs says to the team manager, Dave McNally, "put Larry first up in the lineup."

The manager looks up but says nothing.

"I know he bats third usually, but I want him to have as many chances at bat as he can. I'm told Cavazzini is pitching today – that prick. He could spoil our four hundred if he keeps the ball down.

"You traded him," the manager interjects.

"Yeah. Here's the script. If Larry comes up and gets a hit I want you to pull him out before he bats again. He'll be over the mark. No use taking chances. We need all the publicity we can get to fill the seats, and boy do they need filling. A good ad next year: COME AND WATCH THE ONLY .400 HITTER IN BASEBALL THAT YOU'LL EVER SEE. Maybe nobody hits .400 ever again, what with the longer season and the night games. It should bring in some more fans next year."

"How about buying a good left-handed pitcher in the off-season?" the manager mumbles. "That would help."

"Right. How about a new manager too," the V.P. says in a voice that is meant to be sort of funny, sort of not.

"Larry bats first," the manager says.

He had managed three clubs in the last twelve years and is in his third year in Chicago.

"Right," the manager continues. "But suppose he doesn't get a hit the first time at bat?"

"He does get a hit."

"Just suppose he doesn't hit?"

"Don't bust my chops. He gets a hit. That's it. Six hundred and thirty seven times at bat. Isn't that .401 or something. Fabulous!"

"He gets a hit the first time up – then I yank him."

"He's history, he's kaput, he's out of there. He's gone. He's thinking about next season. Don't be a dumbhead and keep him in. Doesn't matter what he wants."

"But, suppose –. Suppose he doesn't get a hit the first chance."

"Then he stays in. At chance number two, he hits. One for two – a .500 average. .400 plus. You do the math. .401? Then you yank him."

"Suppose he doesn't."

"He does."

"But. Suppose."

"Then he has to bat twice more. The third time at bat he hits. One for three. Still below .400. He has to come up one more time. Batting first, unless it's a perfect game, he comes up four times. Fourth time – another hit. Two for four - .500, he's .400 plus. He's history –"

"Sure, if he makes .400 he's history – he's in the record books. He's good for a big renewal of season tickets."

Dave paused.

"But suppose two for four doesn't get .400?"

"I'm getting heartburn. Give me a Pepto Bismol. Give me an Alka Seltzer."

"But I did the math. That's 3995 something."

"Then, man, unless you squeeze some runs out of those bums –."

"They're the bums you hired –."

"Unless you get some runs, I get a new manager because Larry has to get up another time. The next time he bats – he hits. He's over .400 for sure, right? I don't do math that high."

"Right."

"No more buts. Do it."

Later on, the Cubs manager calls up a friend. "That coaching job with you at the Phillies, is it still open?"

So, here I am. The day starts bad. But I've got lots of time to make it better. There's no early meetings of the team today. That means I can attend an AA meeting. I like the way the meetings always go. You can count on them. "Hello, I'm Larry and I'm an alcoholic. I've been sober for a year, ever since I started to go out with Susan. She turned me around." Then I'd tell about Susan and all and how she made me promise things.

I go to the group that I like the best. Pretty soon I'm up in front.

"Hello, I'm Larry and I'm an alcoholic."

"Hello, Larry."

"I've been sober for three years now, because of Susan. When I met her first she'd been going out with my friend Tony. Then they broke up, and after a while we went out. She said, 'You could be a nice guy if you give up the hard stuff. You could be a nice guy for a girl like me.' 'Like you?' I said. 'Me,' she said, real quick to show she meant it. And I said 'O.K., then.' So, when I was sober for six months Susan said, 'We can get hitched up now, if you want.' I did want, and we're married for a hundred and seventy nine days. I haven't touched a drop. I'm out of town a lot, but I go to meetings whatever town I'm in."

At that I sit down, get lots of smiles, especially from the women, but from the men too, because I guess there are lots of them who would like to have a wife like Susan, someone who will love them and believe in them the way Susan does me.

I feel good when I finish. I know that some of the people there can tell who I am because my picture's been in the paper, Going for four hundred, and stories like that. But nobody at the AA meeting says, 'How's the old boy? How's it going, Larry?' 'Got that sweet swing ready for tonight?' or asks for an autograph, or even says, "Ain't you that ballplayer fellow who's supposed to be hot shit?' Probably

102

somebody knows that I'm right on the edge of being the latest member of the Four Hundred Club. It's all up to tonight. Someone, sure, knows that. But nobody says, 'Good luck.' That's the way it should be. We're just anonymous alcoholics here, not big shots. Or maybe we're all big shots since we are here, because if I go over to some parts of this town, I'll find guys sitting on steps of closed-up stores holding brown paper bags that you know have bottles in them, maybe of muscatel or, if they got a good handout, Early Times. And those guys and sometimes women are really anonymous little shots. Well, for me one day at a time. That goes for tonight, of course. But it really goes for the rest of my life. One day at a time.

Yes, I feel good and the sun is shining, warming my neck. It's lunch time too, and I'm getting that good feeling of being kind of empty and ready to eat. I never had any trouble eating before a ball game. Some guys just eat a dish of pasta or have a couple of bowls of soup. Then, after the game, they have a midnight snack of a T-bone, for instance, or maybe what my Dad used to call a big Dagwood sandwich, before turning in. I don't think that's so good for your sleep. I just eat regular, whatever I want. It doesn't bother me.

I'm thinking of a special reason I want to go to a Chinese Chop Suey joint. There's an old one not far from here I know about, with a neon sign above the door that says "Port Arthur Chop Suey." Of course, the sign won't be turned on at lunch. But that's what it says.

I go into the Port Arthur and don't bother with the lunch specials, one egg roll, fried rice, and a choice. I go right to the dinner menu and order one dish of Beef Broccoli and, you guessed it, Chicken Chop Suey. Susan would approve of these if she were here. "Those are healthy, lots of veggies," she'd say. She'd eat a little of each, not much, because she wants to keep her figure. I'd say, "Have some more, why don't you?" But she'd wave her finger at me and smile and answer, "You know I've got to keep my shape for you. Or else you'll dump me for another girl." "Sure," I'd say, "I'll get two honeys from the DePaul campus, two sexy coeds."

Or else I'd get serious and say, "Susan, I could never find another girl like you. Don't you know I was looking for you all my life?" If I said that, she'd pinch her eyelids and wrinkle her lips in a little smile. And me, sometimes my eyes would get a little wet then because I would really mean it. Then she might say, "All right, then, one more little spoonful of Chop Suey." I'd serve it to her. That feels good when I do it. Gosh, I wish she were here now. We could joke around, talking like that.

Actually, it wasn't the chow I wanted. Why I came over here to Port Arthur is for the time when the waiter brings the bill. That's what I'm waiting for. He knows me, so just as if Susan were here he brings a dish with two fortune cookies on it and two quarters of an orange with the peel on.

I stare at them for a while, the way I do sometimes until Susan will say, "Larry, pick one." Picking one is hard for me. I want a good fortune. But I have to do it. I pick one now. "This one is for me," I say to myself. I unfold the shiny strip and read it. It's a good one. "If you attempt to be Buddha, you will be disappointed, but if you let yourself be Buddha you will be fulfilled. Shanghai Noodle Co." Thank you Shanghai Noodle. I never got a message like this before, a message about Buddha. Never one from Shanghai, always from Peking. The Port Arthur has a new cookie company. Good. I know it could mean anything, but I like to think it means 'O.K. kid, just swing away, don't fight it, it's good news.' "Sounds right to me," Susan would say if I told her that.

The other cookie is Susan's. I hope it has something about me. Crack it open. I don't like hers. "A rolling stone gathers no moss. Peking Noodle Co." I feel cheated. This is one of the old cookies. It doesn't take a genius to see why the Port Arthur Chop Suey has switched to Shanghai Noodle. The Shanghai fortunes are better than Peking Noodle. I feel like I want to ask the waiter, Chin Lee, or whatever his name is, to give me another cookie, one from Shanghai. This one is stale, I could tell him. But I decide, Susan's not here, this fortune doesn't apply to her. Wait until she comes with me when the season's over. Then I'll tell the waiter, "Say, be sure you give us some of the new cookies." For now, I leave the four broken pieces of cookies on the dish. I never eat the cookies. Neither does Susan. But I eat an orange clean from the peel, and pay.

I'm going home to lift some weights and then take a nap. I hope it's not too chilly tonight – I don't like the cold much.

Tony Cavazzini is sitting in the hotel room of Luis Rameriz, the Cardinals shortstop, with Todd Billingsley and Tank Gooding, the one a middle reliever and the other a good catcher. They're playing seven card stud now, though between the four of them they probably know thirty, forty different card games. They're not gambling for money, just for plastic chips. At the beginning of the season they each got a thousand chips, and they can buy more at a store they know if they run out. Tony's are green. They're not playing for money, because Cap, their manager, doesn't allow gambling. But if at the end of the season, they add up how many thousands and calculate them in dollars, who's to blame them?

Luis says, "I'll raise two," just as the phone rings.

Tony says, "Yes" into the receiver.

"Hello, Cap," he says.

He listens for a while.

"Why not?"

"That doesn't make any sense to me."

"Nobody would think that."

"Am I supposed to thank you for sparing me grief? You can keep that."

Tony is getting hot under the collar. The others could see him doodling Xs and Os on the pad next to the phone.

"Cap, I can feel it. I've got it today. I want to go out a twenty game winner."

"I don't care about starting the first game of the playoffs. I've got nineteen. I want to win twenty this season."

"No, I don't think I'm the manager.... I don't think I could run the team better than you do. But have a heart."

"You've got a heart. I *know* you've got a heart.... O.K., then, whatever you say."

"You want me to tell you I agree it makes sense? Let's just leave it at 'whatever you say.'"

"All right. See you in a while."

Luis still holds two blue chips in his hand. But they all look at Tony.

"Cap decided not to pitch me tonight."

"Yeah?"

"He's starting Jack McMaster."

"Well, Jack's rested, that's for sure. He hasn't started in two weeks. And then it was only three innings. He's been sitting in the bullpen with me," Tank says.

Todd chants: "Pitch McMaster and prepare for disaster. Earned run average, 5.67."

"Cap says Jack begged him for one more start before season's end. He says he's rested and he is feeling in the groove." That *is* the way

105

Jack talks, so Cap must actually be telling me what Jack said to him. Besides, Cap is worried that if 'your old pal' Larry gets his hits against you, you might get accused of setting things up for him. Can you imagine that? That stinks. But Cap says that didn't count for much, it's just Jack wanted a game bad. Jack feels good."

"Look at it this way – Cap wants you rested for the playoffs. He probably does."

"He said that."

"Raise two," Luis said. He has a full house. He's pretty sure of taking the pot.

While I was out Susan left a note on the Thinkpad, saying she was in, and where was I? She'll see me at the game. I can tell she had a sandwich for lunch because she left the soggy corners of the crust in the sink, where she rinsed her plate off. I push them down the drain and start the disposal in case there's anything else down there.

I do my weights. I eat a light supper, one of my favorites, a can of Chef Boyardee Ravioli, and then I take a long nap, so when I go to the ballpark I'm good and rested.

Where we players park, there's usually a few girls waiting outside the fence before games. Later, some of them will come and get in the passenger seat when you stop to pull out of the exit if you invite them.

I park my car near the fence. I can see that one girl is being egged on by three of her friends. They're sort of poking and pushing her toward where I am. She's a good looking girl, too. I've seen her before. A redhead. It looks natural on her. She's wearing boots and a miniskirt. Young too. She looks good. She's just a kid. She doesn't know anything. Just one thing and maybe not much about that.

"Larry, my friends say I'm your girl," she calls out. She looks back at them, and they motion to her, meaning, "Go on! Keep going."

"I'm your date tonight," she says.

"Is that so?" I joke with her. I know how to kid girls like her and not get into any trouble. I've done it lots. I think of Susan.

"That so?" I say.

"Oh, yes, yes."

She looks back at her girlfriends, defiant-like. She's going for it now.

"My girlfriends say to tell you if you want some inspiration for tonight's game you can come over here and play with my tits." She leans against the bars of the fence and her tits stick through them.

106

"Come on, I won't bite you." I can see her nipples, hard, pressed through her tight blouse. "Come on, take a little rub for luck, like Aladdin's lamp."

"You'd get me too excited," I tell her. "I won't be able to think of anything but your tits every time I come to bat. Get my meaning?"

One of her girlfriends runs up to her and whispers in her ear. They giggle.

"Take a raincheck then," she says. "Patsy says you can have both of us after the game."

Patsy whispers again.

"Patsy says, 'Anything you want. Anything.' You're the man tonight."

"Thanks for the invite," I say, "But I'm a happily married guy, and I've got a swell wife waiting for me when the game's over. When I drive out, she'll be in the seat next to me. No room for anyone else."

Patsy makes a big smooshy kiss with her lips and tongue and says, "O.K., Larry, we love you. Good luck. We know you'll do great. You're the best."

Maybe Susan wouldn't like it if she heard this kind of talk. I'm hoping that the redhead and Patsy aren't here when we leave because maybe they'd call out things. I won't do anything but slow at the gate and drive right on, and then there won't be any problem.

I pass by the office where Dave, our manager, sits. He's busy word processing, looking at who hits best and who does worst against Tony Cavazzini, I suppose. Of course, I'll be in the lineup, third batter like forever.

Not everyone is in at the locker room yet. Nobody is talking to me. I know why. It's like when someone is throwing a no-hitter, no one talks to him. We haven't had a no-hitter from any of our pitchers this year. But a .400 – that's way bigger than a cheesy no-hitter. They're a dime a dozen. The last time someone batted .400, nobody on the team was even born, unless you count Dave and a couple of the coaches. So, I guess the guys all decided in advance no one talks. I know this is what they're doing because when Pistol Pete Post comes in, he starts right for me with his hand out and I know he is going to say, "Good luck tonight." But Bill steps in front of him and he turns him around and then I see them whispering to him in the corner. Bill goes over to the door to stand there and waylay the rest of the team as they come in.

Dave walks in before it's time to announce the lineups and signals to me to come to the office. I'm still dressed, just sitting in front of my locker, and so I go right in.

"I'm batting you first tonight," he says.

"What happened to third?"

"First means you get the maximum of at-bats. Whenever you get over .400 I'm yanking you. Okay with you?"

He doesn't say, "If you get over .400."

"Whenever."

I have no objection. Not now. Maybe I will when it comes to it. Why make trouble before time?

We go out for batting practice. It's part of the show. I bat longer than I need to or want to when all the others are done, so that if anyone is coming to watch how I'm swinging they'll get a peek.

I look for Susan a few rows in back of the first base dugout. She's not there yet. But the man whose car I hit is there with his kid, and they're waving to me. I go over to the railing and when they come down, a half dozen other kids and dads come down after them.

"This is my boy, Bob," he says. Bob has a baseball and a marker pen.

"Sure," I say. I take the ball. I sign it, "To my pal, Bob!"

Then I have to sign a few programs that other kids are holding out. The security cop catches my eye. I nod, *no*. I don't mind. I put up my hand and flash five fingers. But after I've signed five I do two more. Then I smile and wave. "Gotta go."

Like always, the managers go out with the lineups and they're announced through the sound system. The funny thing is, McMaster is pitching, not Tony. McMaster. That's great. I always hit him. Three, four seasons ago he passed his peak. Maybe I'll get four hits tonight. I've got his number.

Nothing's the way I expected it. Tony's not pitching. I didn't get to visit my mom. I missed Susan all day. I feel kind of grumpy. But as the first batter for the Cards is walking toward the plate I glance around and Susan's slipping into her seat. She's got my mom with her. I never even thought of that. Usually mom would say, "I should come to sit for three hours to watch you at the plate for a total of a minute? Who has that kind of time?" She loves me, I know it. That's just her way. They both wave to me when they see me looking at them.

The announcer says, "Batting first for the Cardinals, number thirty-three, Luis Rameriz, playing shortstop."

On the first pitch he fakes a bunt toward third. On the second he chops a grounder to third. Over to me. Easy out.

One, two, three.

It's strange to start the game with me at bat. I like to sort of size up the pitcher a little before I come up. I watch his warm-ups anyway. Jack looks okay for an old guy.

The first pitch zings in like I haven't seen McMaster throw one for years. Fast. Low-inside, where they always pitch me.

I take another one. Same pitch. Then a set-up pitch, high and away. Now I'm expecting another low and inside. I shuffle a little back from the plate and it comes in where I expect, not where I want. I've got to swing.

The ball squibbles down toward first, twisting inside the foul line. McMaster starts, then looks at the first baseman. First base looks at McMaster. Both start. Both stop. I shoot by them. The second baseman is covering first. The throw comes from behind me. Bang bang. The ball and I arrive nearly together. That big Polack umpire at first is going to call me out, I can just feel it.

"Safe," I hear him say.

Four hundred and something.

It flashes on the screen.

The crowd breaks out in applause. Most people stand. There should've been more fans there to see it. It will replay on the eleven o'clock news. Susan is jumping up and down with her arms in the air. Mom is even applauding. I suppose she's saying, "He made something of himself at last."

What a chicken shit way to break .400. Sure, I know people will say, "You've been robbed plenty of times of sure hits on really hard hit balls. It's about time you got one on a platter." Well, this season, I've gotten some of those too. All I would've asked for was a nice clean line drive through the gap. Even a looper over second base that no one could touch. But not two idiots staring with open mouths at a ball barely moving.

They bring me the ball. I tip my cap, I hand the ball to the first base coach. Dave is on the steps of the dugout. I shake my head no. No pinch runner. When I go back in I'll tell him, "I'm staying in."

"Okay, bask in the glory," he'll say. Tip your cap to the fans. Wave to Susan. I'll pinch hit for you when you come up next, in a couple of innings.

109

The glory is short. Pistol Pete hits a sharp grounder to second. I'm out by a mile. So is he. Dave and I say to each other pretty much what I supposed we would. When we come up again, Todd's hitting in the third slot instead of sixth, and he strikes out.

Three up, three down.

Just before I run back onto the field, I tell Dave, "I'm not going out, not with a hit like that. I'm staying in."

"No way."

I'm out of the dugout now. I call back, "I mean it, Dave."

Two more innings go by. For us, three up, three down. Dave says, "Have a heart, the vice-president will have my hide. He wants a .400 year for you, Larry." Dave insists he's going to pinch hit for me, no buts about it.

I tell him, "If you do, I'll run out on the field and do something horrible. I'll get the umps to call the game forfeit. Back to .39937."

Actually I have no idea how I'd make that happen. But how could Dave know?

"You couldn't do that," he says.

"Maybe I'll expose myself on national television. I'm staying in."

Dave gets on the phone. It's clear the way he's throwing that McMaster's got his stuff. He's rested. He's like his old self. I still can hit him though. I always could. He is revved up for this last game. He's over the hill, but he's got pride. He's going to be tough tonight. We're already three runs down. We've been on the losing end lots of times this season.

So bottom of the fourth, I don't even look at Dave. I slide out my bat and swing in to the batter's circle until McMaster's warmed up.

First pitch. A beautiful swing – the right fielder parks under it. The average is down to .39968. Dave looks gloomy. Batting first, I'll get up two more times. A nice drive, just a single on my third up and maybe I'll go out. I could buy that.

And then I do come up for the third time, in the bottom of the seventh.

McMaster's given three hits, but he's kept the ball low, and they've turned a double play, then the wily bastard picked off the leadoff runner in the sixth inning. Todd connected for a triple next in that same inning. But then he was cut down trying for home on a short fly to left. McMaster is nipping the corners, varying his pitches. At the end of six innings, twenty-one batters have come up, but he's still ended up with

110

leaving zero men on base, just as if it were a perfect game. Our pitcher, South Hadley, is doing fine too, just three runs behind. Three to zip.

Bottom half of the seventh, I bat first. I like to hit with men on. I've got a better percentage when the pitcher doesn't go into a stretch, especially if he's a left-hander like me. This time, two balls, no strikes, Mac comes low, but in the center of the plate, and I smack it in a line that is destined to go right over the head of the second baseman, except that with nobody on he's playing way back, and he leaps and reaches and times it just right and snares it. Nine times out of ten it drops. One for three. Mighty Casey. A moan from the stands.

If things continue like this, I won't get another shot. Hell, how many guys in the history of baseball have hit .399? Maybe no one. That would have been like hitting 59 homeruns before Maris broke Ruth's record. .399 is plenty good. Leads the majors by fifty points, doesn't it? Still, if we leave one runner on, just one, I'll come up again.

We've been starting to hit McMaster hard though, long flies to the outfield, line drives, hard grounders. Following me, Pistol Pete slams a low drive right back toward the pitcher, zinging toward centerfield. Instinctively Mac lunges with his bare hand. It bounces off his thumb. The second baseman pounces on it and almost throws Pete out. But we've got a man on again.

Mac has dropped his glove. He's wringing and shaking his left hand. Naturally there's a conference at the mound.

Out in the bullpen, Tony starts throwing lazily. Cap hasn't asked him to. Cap is out at the mound. Mac is shaking his head "Yes," then "No," then just looking down as Cap and the trainer are inspecting his hand. Cap's staring at Mac's left paw as if it is a raw steak at the Chicago Chop House. Cap's asking him questions. To the last one he shakes, "Yes." He wants to stay in.

"Yes" is the wrong answer. The thumb's no good. The first pitch Jack throws to Matty Biller is a homer, opposite field. Three to two, and I'll get my turn at bat. Jack stands on the mound, his left arm hanging down and twitching uncontrollably. Cap looks out at the bullpen. Tony's throwing. Cap raises his left hand. He wants a lefty to throw too. He doesn't wave Tony away though. The home umpire strolls out. You can tell Cap is saying to the home plate ump something like, "Between us, Jack's through. He's coming out. But let him try a few pitches for his dignity." "Okay," the ump tells Jack, "throw a few. Let's see if you can stay in." Actually Cap is buying time.

111

Jack can hardly throw the ball. If you were up close I bet you'd see his thumb is already twice the size. He takes his time between pitches. The fans, who are never too involved here, lose interest and mob the hot dog and beer stands. Seats are emptying. Cars are leaving the parking lot. No .400 year. Another loss. We're close to a record for total losses, but even at that kind of record, no cigar.

Jack signals Cap. No go. We knew that. Cap walks out, puts his arm around Jack's shoulder and walks with him back to the dugout. Scattered applause. At the top step of the dugout Cap starts to raise his left hand for Sparky Ames to come in, but thinks better of it, because why not end the season a winner, protect the one-run lead. Win the last one before the playoffs. Good psychology. The right hand goes up, Tony puts on his jacket, gets in the cart and in he comes.

The right answer this time. Tony throws three straight strikes. He knows that his fast ball won't be touched unless Jesus Christ is at the plate. The batter is Roger Colwin. He goes down swinging at the third pitch after it's already in the catcher's mitt. Ditto the next batter. Never had a chance. Tony's hurling hard. We're tired. For most of us the season is over. What do they say? – "Slouching toward the final day." That's us.

In the eighth the bottom of the lineup goes down in order.

Opening the last half of the ninth, Dave pinch hits for our pitcher, South Hadley. He's tired too. He's going to the showers. He's glad to be finished. For him the season is in the dumper. He's a divorced guy, and maybe he'll get lucky on his way out of the parking lot. He'll be first out and could score with one of the girls there after all. Our pinch-hitter's Pat Seerey, who came to us in the trade for Tony. He's come up from Triple-A for the end of the season. Someone says he's the grandson of some ancient player, a big beefy man also named Pat Seerey who was in the majors for Cleveland a while and never came to much except that he once hit four homers in one game. But if that's the truth, the genes must have declined in the family because our Pat Seerey is just a scarecrow, all arms and legs.

Maybe he's scared too, being in the majors, with the fans remaining in the stands searching their programs, asking each other, "Who's this hitter?" Sure, he's scared to bat, and so he lays down a bunt. But it's a perfect bunt, down the third base line. The third baseman, even with the bag, is caught sleeping. He hardly moves. The ball stops before he gets to it. He starts to throw, then just walks over to Tony and hands the ball to him. "Sorry," he'd be saying.

112

Now it's Tony and me. He knows how to pitch me. He throws in the 90s. He fires a hard slider that breaks in and low then drops off the shelf. When I swing at a ball in the dirt I feel like a fool.

His first pitch comes in – high, right toward my head. Ninety six miles an hour. I crumple. Imagine ending a .399 season out cold on home plate. That's almost me.

I brush myself off and glare at Tony. He smiles, shrugs his shoulders, mouths, "Sorry." I guess the ball did get away from him. He wouldn't bean me intentionally, would he?

The next pitch is way outside. It looks like he's going to walk me. If I walk, there's no chance for me to make it a two for four day and end the season a winner.

Tony rears back and it comes in just where he wants it, the split finger, low and inside. I don't think. My bat swings. I connect. Sounds good. I'm running, and the first base coach is waving me around. Fuck it, I don't care what happens after I tag first. I speed on, except now I see that Pat Seerey is just getting to second. I guess he didn't get any jump on the ball at all. He just watched it sail out. Maybe he thought the ball would be caught. He's a rookie and he isn't going to let himself be doubled up.

So I slow down a little. The third base coach is frantic. It's the tying run. He's waving Seerey home. I pull up at third not far behind him and watch the relay come in from left field. To the shortstop. To the catcher. Tony is backing up the catcher. Ten feet from the bag Seerey sees the catcher with the ball, guarding the plate. Like a fool he tries to put on the brake, trips over his own big feet, and falls almost at the catcher's toes. Slow motion now. He raises his head a little to look up the way those defeated gladiators in the movies do. The catcher takes a step and stabs the ball into the center of his back. "We who are about to die" – right?

So it's still three to two. But I'm on third. One out. I start to think. The way I figure, two for four should put me over .400. Is it? Or isn't it? It must be close.

Then a cheer goes up from the crowd, what crowd there is. I look up at the Vision Board, and there I am swinging. I look good. The ball darts between the left and center fielders. It shows me looping wide around first. Then the picture goes black and "400.00" flashes on the screen. "Two Hundred and Fifty-Six Hits in Six Hundred and Forty Official at Bats." It comes out on the screen like cannon blasts. "A Club Record Batting Average." "Club Record Hits." "Club Record

113

Singles (Two Twenty One)." It keeps flashing. Susan is waving and jumping around, even hugging my mom. Everyone else is standing around applauding. Time out. The catcher keeps walking down the line after he's tagged Seerey and hands me the ball "That's really great Larry," he says. He means it too. "That goes double for me," Tony says. He's already standing next to me. "You hit the best pitch I had." The third base coach throws his arm around my shoulder. The Vision Board is still flashing. Cap comes out and signals for a pinch runner. Seerey is still lying on the ground. The umps are in a little group talking together. I'm waving at Susan. She's throwing me kisses. Even my mom throws me one. I throw kisses back. I blow kisses to the bleachers. I get more and more excited. I throw my cap into the stands. Maybe some kid will catch it. I hold onto the ball though. It's all swell.

My season is over. Dave puts in a runner for me. I don't want to go to the showers right away. They'll be plenty of reporters and cameras in the locker room in a while. They'll want me to be in uniform for the TV. Everyone comes over and pats me on the back or on my butt or shoulder as I come down the steps of the dugout, the ones that didn't mob me on third. What a pounding. I drape a towel around my neck. Someone brings me a new cap. I sit down next to Dave. It's cold outside, but I'm sweating and in the dugout it's warm.

I sit and sweat while Tony retires the side, a strikeout and a pop up, to end the game. He looks at me and gives me a thumbs up. He's not the kind of guy who thinks about himself. He's glad for me. I give him a thumbs up. That's for him. I'm not thinking of myself now either.

I'm patient with the newsmen and women. The vice-president and Mr. Maguire the owner come into the locker room. Mr. Maguire puts his arm around me and we pose for photos. For the television he says, "Larry, I'm real proud of you. The team didn't come out a winner this year, but fellers" – he's talking to the reporters now – "we've got plans to rebuild the team around Larry here. We've got our eyes on some trades that'll be big for us. This could be a new era. But for today, it's Larry who's a winner. The best player in the game today, bar none."

He sort of playfully punches me in the arm. It's taken a lot of pokes already, but I don't mind. Posing for the reporters, he says to me, "Well I guess you'll be demanding the moon, a big new contract, from Bud here" – meaning the vice president, who is mugging too, putting his hands over his face – "and I'm the guy who's going to end up paying the bill. But I don't care. Today's your day."

He's a big talker, but a pretty cheap guy. For all I know he'll trade me rather than pay my salary. He likes to be way below the salary cap.

At last I get to see Susan, with mom in back of her. Susan is beaming. She kisses me for a long time. There are photographers hanging around still. Actually, I'd like to have copies of the photos of Susan kissing me. I could even frame them and if Susan ever gets sulky with me, I can point to them on the wall and say, "So, who's that classy dame who's giving me the biggest smoocher of the year?" I could make her laugh with that kind of stuff.

Mom says, "Well, you did fine. I brought my own car. I'll just leave you two alone."

"I'll call you up and visit," I say.

I think, it must be terrible for her to be alone, and her still a good-looking woman for her age. It must be really lonely. So, I'm glad for mom. They'll be other breakfasts.

Susan sits next to me when I drive out of the parking lot. Outside the fence a few girls are still around. The red headed kid and her girlfriend Patsy are there. As we come out they unfold a Xerox sign ten feet long. "Larry, you're the best!" it says.

Susan's not mad at all. "They don't know the half of it," she tells me, and tickles me in the ribs.

"We'll get together with Tony tomorrow. He's staying over. But tonight's for us," she says. When we get home, Susan asks me if I want to turn on the Sports News and see myself hitting a triple again. But I had enough of that.

Now that I look back on this day, from the time I got up this morning to the time we went to sleep and then when I woke up this morning it had been a perfect twenty-four.

It's the next morning. The season is over. I'm lying in bed. Susan brings me a protein drink with a banana in it.

I joke with her. "I guess you think I need that to regain my strength."

That means she should come back to bed to see if the protein is working.

But Susan is already getting dressed and putting on makeup.

"It's ten o'clock already," she says. "I told Tony we'd come over and pick him up. We'll have a few hours before driving him to the airport."

115

It's a fun day. We laugh a lot. Wherever we go there's someone who recognizes me and knows what I've done. One woman comes up to us in a bookstore. With her husband standing right there she tells me, "We watched the game on TV and when you made the triple he got so excited we did it right there on the couch and he didn't even take his little blue pill."

"Once in a lifetime," the husband mumbles shyly. Later, Tony says, "Did he mean you, Larry, or himself?"

After we drop Tony off at Midway, Susan picks up an evening paper.

When we get home, we open it to the sports section. On the left column there is a nice op-ed by Les Smalley, the sports columnist, celebrating me for staying in the game after my first cheap hit.

But there was a bigger headline in the center. "TRADE RUMORS SWIRL AROUND CUBS .400 HITTER. Rumors that Larry Slade will be traded to the Yankees or Red Sox were all around both cities tonight." Chicago's mayor is quoted as saying, "A trade is unthinkable. Larry Slade is a municipal treasure."

"The mayor doesn't pay the bills," Susan says. "That's capitalism for you. Buy at the dip. Sell at the high."

So, was this my peak?

Maybe I'll never hit .400 again. Did anyone but Cobb do it more than once? But hitting .400 was not what made my peak.

Not with Susan as my wife.

ONE HUNDRED PROOF

Everyone tried to talk Jason out of drinking. One intervention followed another. His mom and dad. Aunts and uncles. Friends. Teachers. His manager and coaches. The team owner. Unhappy sighs by his wife Julie. Uncertain sidelong glances from his boys. But nothing worked. He was like a stainless steel mint julep cup, impervious to all the advice poured into him.

After all, he was twenty-six years old and had already been drinking steadily for fifteen years. Even as a freshman in the Mayor Jimmy Walker High School in New York City, he was a steady drinker, as well as a pitcher that major league scouts knew about. He was signed by the Texas Rangers out of high school.

During his one year in the minors he kept right on drinking. At twenty he was brought up. The team owner made a little celebration on the morning that he signed his rookie contract. The ink was still wet when Jason plucked a full bottle of Dom Perignion 1995 out of the ice bucket and drained half of it before he set it down.

The general manager, Pete Garrett, and Churchill "Bucky" Downs, the Ranger manager, egged him on. They liked what they thought was his wild boyish exuberance for the game. They didn't realize that it was the bubbly he was wild about. And they didn't have the slightest idea that for him the champagne was just an aperitif to begin the day.

Jason drank everything except hair tonic. Every time he heard of a new liquor he was in a frenzy of expectation until he tried it. He was like a surfer waiting for the next perfect wave, and he rode many a bottle to the shore. Before he met and married Julie, he had brief flings with a few girls, but even the dimmest bimbos eventually sensed that his real pleasure came with booze. Barely had he rolled off a girl before he'd be saying, "OK, fine. Let's have a drink."

His first year in the majors he was used sparingly, but still made a 7 and 1 record. Bucky Downs often stared dubiously at him when he left the bench periodically to spend a few minutes replenishing his energy in the locker room.

"You're not going to last," Downs would say ruefully, "with all this drinking. You don't eat. Skinny as a rail. You'll burn out, sure, you, with all your talent. You could be something, you know?"

"Ah, Bucky," he'd say, "Orange juice for vitamins and gin for energy. I'll be all night."

Downs considered sending him to sit in the bullpen where he wouldn't have access to his locker. He actually tried it once. But his rookie had already stashed a bottle of Captain Morgan's spiced rum at the bottom of the ball box out there. What's the use? Next game Jason was back in the dugout.

At spring training of his sophomore year he tore up the opposition. There was no point in bringing him along slowly. He was already *there*. He started the season ahead of Larry Ensor, who had been number one the past five years, and he threw a two-hitter in a complete game. Between innings he polished off a bottle of Benedictine and Brandy.

That year he won twenty-two games and had an earned run average of 1.75.

So it went, year after year. No one knew whether he took more pleasure in the strikes he threw or the bottles he drained. He didn't know himself.

He was always happy, good with reporters, patient with fans. He signed autographs at Children's Hospital. He appeared with the local mayors of nearby towns at teenage gatherings to preach against drugs and unprotected sex. He got an award from the city of Houston for "Distinguished Community Service." He celebrated this honor by buying a bottle of Bushmills Single Barrel. The award was dumped in a drawer, but the glorious Irish Whiskey was tossed down with memorable pleasure.

"How long can this go on?" Julie would say. "On the outside, you're fine. Everyone loves you. You don't cat around. You come right home after the games. You play with the boys. You barbeque for the neighborhood. You don't pass out at parties. You don't even slur your words. You're perfect. But you must be killing yourself on the inside. How long can a liver last with this abuse? When will your kidneys go? Your heart? Jay, I love you, and I don't want to lose you. And what about the boys growing up without a dad?"

When she talked like that he'd put his arm around her shoulders and kid her a little.

"Say, don't worry. Buck says the same. But look how fit I am. Haven't I posted a better record every year? I'll get thirty, thirty-five games next season, the first since Denny McLain."

"And look what happened to him," Julie answered, twisting up her face.

"Not me," he said. He meant it too.

118

But with all the pounding from everyone, a little doubt crept in eventually. He liked to pitch, he liked the game, he wanted to last. He didn't like the talk about his falling apart all at once either.

Offseason he sometimes played golf with Father Malachy, a big mick who was a heavy hitter off the tee.

On the fourth hole, the priest spoke up.

"Even a good Irishman like John Daly was done in by the booze," Father Pat said, teasing him. "How can I say it? If it got to Daly, what will drink do to a godless Jew?"

How could a dumb joke like that cause a sudden conversion when nothing else had made the slightest dent? Of course, it couldn't. But the kaleidoscope had turned, old pieces fell into a new picture and everything seemed altered. Saul had been knocked of his horse.

On the way home, Jason stopped, as he always did after 18 holes, at Hernando's Hideway.

"What'll it be?" Hernando asked when Jason hoisted himself on a stool. Jason never knew what he was going to have. Which bottle would gleam and twinkle at him this day? He let his eyes slide from one to another, all the pretty bottles, brown and crystal and chartreuse green and brilliant yellow – a carnival of liquid glass.

"Just give me a coffee," he said, without meaning to.

"Irish coffee? Fra Angelico? Bailey's – double shot? What'll it be?" Hernando always waited anxiously for the moment of the day's revelation. All his other customers were predictable. Jason never. He could just as easily ask for a Jack Rose or a Stinger as a shot of Grey Goose.

"Black coffee," Jason said. Again, his voice didn't seem to come from him.

Hernando wiped an invisible spot of water on the bar.

"Coming up," he said finally. Bewildered.

The coffee was stale and burned. It tasted like mud mixed with sewer water. But he drank it down to the last drop.

A special room in Jason's house was consecrated to alcohol. Money had been no object, and Jason had collected the rarest bottles in the world – a sour mash once stored in Andrew Jackson's cellar, a square hand-blown flask of 140 proof black molasses rum made in Jamaica by slaves, a bottle of cognac that remained in Napoleon's cellar when he left Elba, twenty or more handblown bottles of grappa, a concoction made in Peru from coca leaves, so old that no one knew its name, a

119

magnum of Pol Roger from Churchill's stock…a precious museum of extraordinary drinks.

But Jason didn't treat these as a museum, catalogued, labeled, and untouched. He drank them all. Each rare bottle he consumed was replaced by a new one. A hundred and fifty-seven bottles of such rarity still remained. But many specimens at least as rare as these had been enjoyed.

Julie saw him come in the front door and followed him into the temple of alcohol.

One glance was all he took.

"Call Sotherby's," he said, and tell them to auction off the whole lot. We'll give the proceeds to the Society for the Prevention of Alcohol Abuse by Minors."

"All?" she asked in wonder.

"Well, keep the Napoleon for a souvenir," he said.

"I love you, Jay," she whispered, but with a catch and a strain of doubt in her voice that only she heard.

She might as well have doubted if the seasons would continue or that day would follow night.

The brandy stood all alone, unattended and unseen on a shelf. November, December, January, February passed. March came and went. He never touched another drop. He didn't take up smoking, he never had used drugs. He didn't begin to chase women or haunt the race track. Everyone scrutinized him to see what he would substitute for John Barleycorn, but he didn't put anything in its place. He just stopped drinking. Period.

He gained a few pounds, but he ran daily and lifted weights, and he stayed in very good shape. Bucky and Pete came to see him, and both pressed their strong conviction that he looked healthier than ever. They ventured to say that a couple of more pounds might make his fastball snap even more as it rose toward the plate.

"Who was the last pitcher to win forty games?" Garrett wondered. But that record was so far back in the infancy of the game that no one knew the answer. Perhaps Albert Spalding or Iron Man McGinnity? "Walter Johnson never made forty, did he?" Bucky wondered dubiously. "Or Christy? Who was that guy with a name like a president?"

Within a couple of days, in the sports section of the Houston papers an article appeared, "The First Forty Game Winner?/Jason Glassman Aims to be the First 40-Game Winner in Modern Baseball/Future Hall of

Famer in Best Shape of His Life." Garrett was a past master at planting good public relations stories in a willing press.

Everyone went to spring training with high hopes for Jason in the coming season. Jason simply *went*, the way he always did, just to pitch, expecting nothing.

During the winter the Rangers acquired a left-hander, Bill Blaine for Ensor. With Blaine and Jason and Frank Turk, a four-season reliable hurler, the team seemed headed for the World Series.

Jason ran and stretched and sat in the whirlpool and got massages. He tossed the ball around and played pepper. He warmed up with a utility catcher. An assistant coach filmed his delivery and when the coaches studied the films his motion looked good, he was throwing exactly as he had for the last seven years, without the slightest strain. He threw strikes with the same ease and unerring accuracy as ever. All the pitches were there – fast ball, split finger, fork ball, slider, changeup, curve, "Say," he joked once, "Didn't that Albert Spalding fellow have what he called a dew drop curve? I might just get me a dewdrop too." In the old days everyone would assume that he'd be drinking Tullamore Dew that evening, but now they all believed that he really meant what he said.

That was the most enthusiastic he had ever gotten over his pitching. Everyone smiled. It seemed like a good sign.

They were going over to Tampa to play their first spring game with the Yankees.

Bucky said, "Just give me three innings, I don't want you to do any more today. Three innings. That'll be just fine."

"Sure, Buck," he said. "No problem."

In the top of the first inning the Texas left fielder Red Carter smacked a solo home run off Clemens. So even before Jason took the mound he was already in the lead.

He had said "no problem." But there was a problem.

He threw his fast ball on the first pitch. But the ball didn't jump, and Jeter sent it over the fence. Jason teased the second batter with a slider that nicked the top outside corner of the plate, but the batter sent a screaming line drive into right center field that didn't get chased down until he stood on third.

The Ranger catcher came out to the mound. "Relax," he advised.

"I am relaxed," Jason said.

"You all right? Arm all right?"

"Sure."

121

"Two lucky shots."

"Sure."

"O.K., settle down."

"Right," Jason agreed. I'm going to throw my Spalding dewdrop curve. I've been practicing. Watch out for it."

"Let's go."

"Here it comes, the dewdrop," Jason thought as he wound up.

He reared back, and as he came forward, he heard a pop. It was loud enough for the infielders to hear it too.

Bucky came out, looking worried. The third baseman came over too.

"How's the arm?" they both asked.

"Fine," he said, but when he tried to lift it to show that nothing was wrong, he couldn't raise his arm above his shoulder. It didn't hurt, not then, he just couldn't get it higher.

"Take a rest," Bucky said.

Not even one out. A problem.

Doc Traynor – the trainer – worked on him for a week. The problem was, the old arm didn't seem the same. It felt dead.

After years in the majors he had acquired some savvy even without trying to, and now he began to use it. On his next spring outing, he toiled through three scoreless innings, mixing up the pitches skillfully, throwing low. He gave up six singles, but double plays saved him. In another game the Rangers piled up a big score early, so no one paid any attention to the four runs he allowed in three innings.

But Bucky wasn't fooled. For the first time in six years, Jason didn't start on opening day.

Jason pitched the third game of the season. He went six innings and allowed three runs. No one mentioned that this was against the previous year's last place team, with the lowest per-game run production in the league.

After that he bumbled on, mostly getting pulled after a few innings. But the Ranger batters were tearing up the League and they often came from behind to save him from taking the loss.

Years ago, baseball writers coined the phrases, "middle reliever" and "closer" for pitchers who were expected to go for only a few innings in relief. Now a smart aleck sports writer for the Dallas paper started to call Jason the "early starter."

"Good thing that Frank has really come into his own and Blaine has blossomed," Garrett said to his manager in midseason. They didn't mention Jason, but he was always in back of any estimates they made of the team's chances to make the playoffs.

Blaine and Turk both made the all-star team. Blaine was picked to start. Jason was left home. He had a won-lost record of three and six.

At the start of the second half of the season, the Rangers were only one game out of first place in the western division. That was when the wise guy from the Dallas paper started a new slogan. It was hardly an original one.

"Turk and Blaine, then pray for rain," the reporter chanted in his column. Sometimes he'd throw in his snappy "early starter" phrase to needle Jason.

But Jason wasn't needled. For all anyone could see, he remained unperturbed.

Even on the occasions when Downs strolled out the mound to take the ball from him, he showed no emotion. "Sure, Buck," he'd say and hand him the ball with a gentle smile.

He was tranquil. He remained sober. On off days, when he wasn't on the road or didn't go to the ballpark, he liked to sit in the sun and read books by Rick Warren, Henry Cloud, and all those other positive thinkers from California. He listened to Dr. Phil and Dr. Laura. He talked at length to his children about achieving calm. He said that he had been too frenzied for too long, and he gradually withdrew from his community appearances.

For weeks after Jason first went on the wagon, Julie monitored the old brandy bottle that gleamed on the sideboard in solitary grandeur. It always remained sealed with a big gob of red wax stamped with a bee at its mouth, and soon she passed it by without even seeing it.

Following the all-star break Jason lost three straight games. It could have been five, but he was saved by good long relief jobs and late Ranger rallies. His 3-9 was enough of a disaster.

The Dallas pain in the ass chortled, "Turk and Blaine, then pray for rain," and now regularly added little nagging couplets like: "When Jason Glassman gets his starts, he's hardly in when he departs."

"I don't know, Jay," Garrett said, "we've done everything we can. The x-rays showed nothing. The CT scans showed nothing. No bone chips, no tears, no nothing. The blood work proved there was no infection. Whirlpools don't help. Massages do nothing. Ice, the same. Heat, no difference."

123

"Don't forget the hypnotist and the Prozac," Glassman added, wanting to help.

It didn't help. "Yes, and the aroma therapy and those spooky DVDs with flutes and bells. Nothing's worked. You've tried it all."

"Sure did," Jason said.

"Nothing's wrong, but everything is," Pete said flatly.

"Good that Frank and Bill are throwing so good," Jason remarked.

"The trouble is, Jason – I mean the trouble for me as general manager – is that when you won thirty-two last season we signed a five-year contract for ninety million, including bonuses. I'm thinking now that this is a time when we ought to discuss you'll take a cut, renegotiate the contract. What you say? We've been good to you, haven't we? But you're not doing good for us. Everyone thinks you're never going to be what you were again. That's not ninety million pitching. Sure, you could get your lawyer and agent and union rep in, and make a big stink in the newspapers, but frankly you're in no position to get a lot of fan support. They're pretty down on you. I guess you know that."

"I've heard the boos," Glassman stated.

"Well, I just wanted to get you thinking about it."

"Yeah, I could think about it. I've sort of been expecting you'd bring it up. I see where you're coming from, and it's probably the right thing."

"Good, we'll talk. I'll have another agreement drawn up for you to look at. I've already gotten our attorney started on it. It'll be ready in a week or so."

"O.K. Sure."

"And," Garrett continued, "I wanted to tell you myself – we've always gotten along, haven't we? – that Bucky's sending you out to the bullpen. Maybe you'll give us an inning as a closer when we need it."

"I don't mind," Jason replied.

Turk and Blaine continued to win most of their games. Garrett brought up a couple of young hurlers from the minors and everyone was happy whenever Jason pitched a ninth inning without the roof falling in. He even won a home game. He closed out the Angels in the top of the ninth with the California team ahead six to one. Then the Rangers scored six big runs in the bottom of the ninth to turn what looked like a hopeless loss into a sweet victory. Jason kept this 4-9 record to the end of the season.

124

The Rangers had the worst won-loss record of the four division leaders, even worse than the wild card team. But they were the division leaders, and they were in the playoffs.

Following the close of the regular season, Jason walked into Garrett's office.

Right away he announced: "I'm here until the end of the playoffs or the series, if we get into it. Then I'm through."

"Quitting?" Garrett's eyes opened like dollar signs in a cash register.

"Yeah, my agent will be in. Already told him. He'll make settlement. I don't much care what it is. But he's counting on his percentage, and he deserves it."

"That's decent of you," Garrett answered. "Sure, we can work things out, be fair all around."

An early evening banquet was scheduled before the first playoff game. A good meal, light drinking, then early to bed for the players. Everyone was invited, all the staff and the office workers, the advertising agencies, and of course the wives of the players and the players themselves.

At home before the dinner Jason mentioned to Julie, "I told Pete I'm quitting the team after the last game."

"I'm glad," she said. "we've got good investments, money's no problem, the kids' colleges are banked, the house is paid. We'll be fine. It'll be great to have you with me all the time. It's what I dreamed of."

"Me too," he said. He went out to read in the early October sun.

That night everyone who ate the Lobster Newburgh got food poisoning. If they also ate the salad with the creamy dill dressing, that too was contaminated, and they had a serious double dose. Those who ate only the lobster crowded the Houston emergency rooms during the night. Some were diagnosed with appendicitis due to their white blood counts, and had an appendix removed by a first year resident who was grateful to have a chance at a simple surgery. Those banqueters who ate both the lobster *and* the creamy dill were all hospitalized for excruciating pain and serious side effects. One woman had a stroke during her intake.

Jason ate both the Lobster Newburgh and the salad. He even ate Julie's dill salad, which she hadn't touched.

125

Driving home after the banquet, he suddenly pulled over to the curb, shut the engine off, and fainted.

"You could be having a heart attack," Julie said, when she got him into the back seat so she could drive. "We should go to the hospital."

"Take me home," he groaned. "I'll be OK if I can just lie down."

"You sure?"

"Just get me there."

She did.

By then he was doubled up and she had to roll him into bed in his clothes.

"Want some Pepto-Bismol?" she suggested. "I'll see what I've got."

"Sleep," he mumbled, "just sleep. Please," he said. And he instantly curled up.

She slid under the covers next to him and held him. Hearing him breathe quietly she drifted off to sleep herself.

Sunrise woke her.

Jason was already shaved and dressed. He was combing his hair, and he started to whistle when he saw in the mirror that she was awake. He looked perfectly fit.

"I guess it was just a stomach bug," she said, "but you sure had me worried last night."

"Thanks for getting me home. I'm fine now."

The phone rang.

Julie got it and listened for a few minutes.

"No, he seems fine," she said. Then, "Yes, he did, but he's up and dressed. I'll tell him."

"What?"

"It was Louise from the front office. The staff is calling everyone to find out who's sick and who isn't."

"What do they say?"

"Food poisoning. The lobster and salad. Serious. Half the team's in the hospital. Now I can relax, you weren't having a heart attack. Imagine, food poisoning. Lucky it didn't hit you bad."

"I fainted last night."

"But you got over it better than any one else."

"Iron man," he joked.

Bucky called then.

"So you're in the pink," Jason said.

"You too," Downs replied. "I guess we were both lucky to eat the Delmonicos."

"I ate the Lobster. And the salad. And I had one swift pain in the ass last night, but I guess I passed it out. I had an antidote."

"Too bad Frank and Bill and half the team don't have your constitution. They're both knocked out. How's your arm?"

"Feels swell," Jason said brightly. "Yes, feels swell. Feels like the old arm."

"I'm starting you tonight," Buck said. "You've got to go as many innings as you can. We really need you to get us through until Frank and Bill are back."

"I can do that," he told the manager with the same calm assurance as always.

"Thanks. I know about your talk with Pete. Just do what you can."

He hung up.

"I'm starting tonight," he told Julie matter-of-factly.

He gave her a kiss and hugged her a little. "I'm going out for a little," he said.

"Want some breakfast first? Or maybe you should give your stomach a rest?"

"That's it, that's what I'll do," he said as he went to the door. "Rest the old stomach."

In a while Julie got up and showered and put on sweats, thinking she'd go for a run, then get a protein drink and a banana for herself.

When she walked through the house and passed the sideboard, she stopped. She took a few steps back. There it was. Chunks of red wax lay on the wood. The bee was broken into bits. The brandy that had rested in the bottle for almost two hundred years was gone.

Hernando didn't open his doors until nine, when the truck drivers would take their first break of the day for a couple of beers and a mug of clam juice.

While he waited for the Hideaway to open Jason got a cold quart of Bud in a 7-11. The bottle made a little sigh when he twisted off the cap and got started on his breakfast.

Hernando was surprised to see him push the door open, the first time in months. The first thing Jason said was, "You know, old brandy's the best antibiotic. Let's have a Pimm's Cup."

"Good to see you back, buddy," Hernando said.

Jason didn't rush. He knew just how to do it. Slow and steady. Without haste, without rest. Who said that? W.C. Fields?

127

He sipped the Pimm's for a half hour. Then it was time for his morning coffee – with a double Galliano. He finished off the morning with a Ramos Gin Fizz that he had taught Hernando to make. It was a fine morning.

It all went down so nice and smooth on top of the brandy. Food poisoning never had a chance.

By noon he was ready to go down to the club for a massage and some easy weight lifting. As Doc Traynor kneaded his arm, he could feel the fire. His arm glowed again. In his imagination he beheld a vision of a *pousse café* – seven distinct stripes of different colored liquor, one above the other, held in place by their different specific densities. It was like a prism, radiant and dazzling. He knew where to get one too, and he went.

When he came back to the house, still pulsating from that astonishing concoction, Julie hugged and petted him. She didn't mention the brandy. Could he eat something, just a bit, before the game?

Of course he could. The same as he had had for years – until this year – a can of tuna fish with bread-and-butter-pickles. That hit the spot.

Bucky called. Julie answered.

"He's in great shape….No, no pains….Yes, I'm sure, the best I've seen him in months….He's getting ready to come to the park now….I'll tell him."

The team the Rangers fielded that night was one of the strangest in history. Lucky for Jay, Luis, his favorite catcher was purely a meat and potatoes man. He was built like a brick wall, and in previous seasons he was the only one of the battery who could handle all of Jason's pitches. The infield was shot to hell. One of the outfielders who had been converted years ago had to come in to play third, which meant that a pinch hitter had to go out in right and a utility infielder took over at first. The regular second baseman was in there. He had picked at the salad. He could play even though he was still reeling a bit. A rookie had been activated from the minors at the end of the season and was in center, looking nervous.

In the locker room, Jason got ready for his warm-ups with a beautiful water glass half full of pure crystaline Stolichnaya pepper vodka. "Vodka for nourishment and pepper for energy," he whispered happily to himself. As he sipped, his skin came alive. When he threw his first warm-up pitch, his good old fastball, it jumped up so quickly at the last second that it whistled over the catcher's glove and nicked his left ear.

Luis put on a mask after that.

All the pitches worked. The split finger dove down and out. The fork ball crackled. The fast ball leaped. The change up drifted in three-quarters speed. It was a dance.

"Looks good," Bucky told Glassman when the pitcher came into the dugout, put on his jacket, and dropped down next to the manager. "Try to keep it down," he said, meaning the ball. "Let's hope the infield holds it together."

Just before he trotted out to the mound, Jason slipped into the locker room for one sweet swallow of Calvados. It tamped down all the rest just perfectly.

His joy was so great that on his way out to the mound, he told Luis, "Just watch yourself. I'm throwing it all tonight. Do your best." And he showed him a few finger signals.

He threw them all. First fast balls, one after another, 93, 94, 96 miles an hour – jumping.

By the third inning he started on the slider and the split finger and the fork ball.

He hardly needed an infield. At the end of three innings the catcher had gloved three foul balls that went almost straight up. A soft fly to the short stop and another to the rookie in center. Strikeouts otherwise.

No one said anything to him in the dugout. Only half the team was there anyway.

In the fourth, Jason called Luis out to the mound. A happy thought had come to him in the john between innings as he downed a shot of Canada's best rye.

Jay floated a knuckle ball that came in like a rhumba, sliding back and forth. He had practiced the pitch but never used it in a game. Then a screwball that he had learned from watching old films of Carl Hubbell and Fernando Valenzuela.

In the fifth inning he trotted out the Albert Spalding dewdrop, which dropped like a stone, cutting a diagonal from the batter's waist to his knees, then hitting the dirt just behind the plate. A thimble of sloe gin lay behind that pitch.

After that it was the whole shebang – fastball, dewdrop, slider, knuckler, fork, changeups, curve, brush back, screwball, dewdrop, one

129

after the other, a rainbow of pitches, a dazzling prism, a *pousse café* of baseballs.

Through nine innings he gave up four hits in all. If the regular center fielder had been in, it would have been only three. The ball was swerving like a corkscrew. He walked three. What did it matter? Not a runner crossed the plate. He got a two run lead in the fifth and he made it last.

By the seventh inning stretch everyone in the park knew. Jason was there again. The fans started to chant his name, Jason Glassman. Jason Glassman, as if it held a magic spell in it. Everyone knew. This was the best game they would ever see.

There should have been high jinks in the locker room, but there was a hush. No one even looked straight at him or slapped his back. He seemed untouchable. It had been better than Don Larsen's perfect game, the best game ever pitched from the day in 1845 that Alexander Cartwright of the New York Knickerbockers had invented modern baseball.

Finally, Jason himself broke the silence.

"Isn't there any champagne around?" he asked. "A little flute of Dom Perignon 1996 would go down swell just about now."

It wasn't a '96, but Bucky did produce a Dom Perignon. It popped just like a Glassman fastball.

The next day Jason came in to relieve Frank Turk at the beginning of the seventh. The fans started chanting right away. Jason Glassman. Jason Glassman.

Blaine wrapped up the division playoffs. Three straight.

Even the creep for the Dallas paper put his finger in the air, got the sentiment of the fans, and when the Rangers sailed through the league playoffs, he penned a new rhyme: "Glassman, Turk, and Blaine drive the other teams insane."

The World Series capped the season off. Not surprisingly, Frank and Bill were both tired. They'd pitched steadily all season. Jason started the series and won. Then the Rangers lost two straight with a day for travel between. Jason pitched on three days rest and shut out Kansas City. Another loss and then a win for the Rangers. The series went to seven. In the deciding game Jason relieved Blaine in the sixth and got the win. It was the first time since Detroit's Mickey Lolich that anyone had won three in a series. Series MVP.

On the field after the game the Rangers owner, Pat McKinley, and Garrett and Downs pulled Jason into their circle to receive the trophy, arms around each other's shoulders.

"What a year," Garrett said. "What a year."

"What a season we'll have next year," Pat McKinley said.

"Well," Jason put in, "I told Pete I'm quitting after this season."

Garrett was quick.

"Hey Jay," he said, putting his arm back around the pitcher's neck, "I'm tearing up the new contract we made. I already cleared it with Pat. Ninety million for five years – guaranteed."

Jason remained doubtful. Maybe he'd just quit.

Bucky said, "We wanted to give you a special bonus too. So we got a scout out, not a baseball scout but an auction scout, and we've found a case, a whole case, of Jack Daniels 1890 quarts, up for bids in an auction in Hartford."

"Really?" Jason said tentatively.

"And," Bucky paused. "They once belonged to Sinatra. What do you think of that? Mia Farrow got them in the divorce."

"No kidding?"

"And," Bucky paused meaningfully again, "the case is signed by Joey Bishop –"

"And?"

"– Peter Lawford –"

"Yes? –"

"And Dean Martin –"

"Dean too?"

"Sammy Davis –"

"And of course –"

"Yes, by Frank himself."

"Well, that's just wonderful," Jason said. "It would make a great beginning for my new museum."

"It's already down in the locker room," Pat said to his star pitcher.

"What I say –" Jason started, his eyes sparkling and lips glistening,

"– What I say is, why don't we go down and try a bottle right now? Sure, one little case won't last the whole of next season, but there's the seed of forty wins in it, and we might as well get it planted."

They did get started. Later they continued their celebration at Hernando's. McKinley, Garrett, and Downs got completely sloshed trying to match Jason drink for drink. After midnight, he had to pour the three of them into the back seat of his car and drive them home. Friends don't let team owners and managers drive.

A YANKEE DOODLE

Conrad Trevor's wife Eleanor left him three weeks ago. Since then he has written nothing, not a happy state for a man who lives by his word processor. He's a writer who stopped writing. But he can still drink coffee, and besides, it is July 3, his forty-first birthday. So on a summer morning he is sitting at a Starbucks on Broadway and 114th Street under a green umbrella having a mocha latte.

Conrad feels sour. At a nearby table is a man in his forties with a closely-trimmed beard and rimless glasses. He looks like Trotsky. He wears an expensive work shirt. An intellectual phony, Conrad decides. He is reading *Radical Islam and America in Crisis*. Conrad reflects, Eleanore left him for a guy like that, a Columbia professor, an Islamo-Fascist. This could even be the man.

A young couple bring their coffees out to the patio. The young woman looks like a mousy graduate student. The man is carrying a big gift-wrapped carton. He wears a white shirt with no tie and a cheap suit like those worn by the middle-eastern men Conrad has seen on TV. As they pass the bearded man, Conrad believes that a sign passes between the three. The man with the book had stationed himself there to await their arrival. The bland girl goes over to the man's table. He removes his rimless glasses.

"May I borrow this cinnamon shaker?"

"Why yes, of course. You may keep it." Conrad thinks that maybe there was a message fastened to the bottom of the shaker.

He has a vision of what all this means. The professor has seduced her and drawn her into an anti-American plot. She is a terrorist dupe. The Arabic man is her contact.

The man in the workshirt closes his book and leaves. At their table the couple are deep in conversation, their heads bent so closely toward each other that their brows almost touch. The young woman looks at her watch, then reaches into her backpack and takes out what could be a checkbook or a pad. She writes something, then tears the page out and hands it to the man. He too looks at his wristwatch, then stands up and leaves without so much as a goodbye.

The girl dutifully cleans the table with a napkin and takes the coffee cups and tray over to the trashbin. When she returns to the table she sits and folds her hands demurely before her. She puts pink lipstick on and fluffs her hair. She looks younger, prettier.

Conrad and the girl wait fifteen minutes. Suddenly her face blooms into a broad smile of delight to greet a figure rumbling into view. He is slender and walks gracefully with long, loping strides. He wears a baseball cap with NY in gothic lettering on it. Beneath the cap, blond curls flow out. He wears a polo shirt with a golden fleece on it, smart slacks, and expensive walking shoes. The girl dances into Conrad's view, throwing her arms joyfully around the man's neck.

"Oh Connie," she squeals, "I've been so longing to see you."

He circles her waist and swings her back and forth exuberantly.

Conrad puts it together. Somehow, Connie is the terrorist girl's target.

Conrad remembers Connie's face – he's seen it on the sports pages. He's one of the rookies for the Yankees. Something is up. The story is unfolding inside his head.

She must have been instructed on how to meet him. On TV she studied his performance at the plate and second base. She had memorized every scrap of information about him.

She sat in a sports bar where it's known he goes sometimes. On the third night he walks into the bar. The Angels are playing the Mariners. She sits down next to him.

"I just adore the Angels," she says to him.

Connie sees a pretty girl talking to him.

"You've seen the Angels – in person?"

"Oh yes," she says animatedly. "Dozens of times."

"So you lived in L.A.? Why, I did too. Where were you?"

"In Glendale," she answers.

"I'm from Pasadena. Grew up there."

"Then we were practically neighbors!" she says gleefully. "What luck to meet another Southern Californian in this big city!"

"I'd say it is!" Connie replies. He adds, "I'm with the Yankees now, but I always figured I'd play for the Angels."

"Oh," she says, "You play baseball? You've got a perfect physique for a baseball player."

"Baseball, sure. I've been brought up from Columbus. Sure, I'm a baseball player."

"Oh my," she says with a sudden shyness. "And I'm talking to you. I never talked to a professional baseball player before, a real professional."

"I'm just a rookie," he says, "Only three years out of UCLA."

"You're a Bruin? I'm UC too," she cries. "A Golden Bear from Berkeley. But I had two cousins who went to UCLA. They loved it. And of course you've got a better baseball team than Cal."

"Well, we beat Cal the last three years straight."

"Oh gosh," she continues, "I have to come here again when the Yankees are on TV, so I can see you in action. This is the first time I've ever come to a sports bar. You know how fresh the guys at a bar can be – that's what my girlfriends tell me. But when I heard that the Angels were playing I got up my nerve to give it a try, I wanted to see them so bad."

"Stick next to me, I won't let anyone bother you," he assures her. "My name is Connie Thorp."

"Mine's Ellie. It's sure nice to meet you."

"Wouldn't you like to have something to drink?" he asks. "I'm having a Miller Lite. Say, did you ever see the Miller factory off the 210?"

"I never did, but I'd like to. Anyway, I'll drink a diet Coke."

He tries to pay for the Coke, but she hands a five-dollar bill to the bartender.

"What are you doing in New York?" he inquires.

"I'm a graduate student at Columbia," she tells him. "New York's a really cold place though. And some of the professors can be kind of leftist."

"Wow," he tells her, "it's just like being back in school, back at home, to talk to you. Did you ever go surfing at Huntington Beach?"

"My guy friends did, a lot," she says, "but the waves were too big for me there."

"I did the Wedge in Newport," he brags.

They chat on like this for a while. In answer to his questions, she admits that she had gone to Disneyland, Knotts Berry Farm, the Newport Fun Zone, and had burgers at Tommy's.

"You sure look fit," he says.

"You too. The Yankees are my second favorite team," she admits.

"Then 'I'm lucky to be a Yankee'," he replies.

She says that she must be lucky too because they met each other, and she gives him her cell phone number.

After a few days Connie calls to invite her to a Yankee-Seattle game. Nice seats, just in back of the Yankee dugout, where the wives sit. Once there, she meets some of the wives too, and they all get along very well.

135

After the game he takes her back to her apartment and takes a chance and kisses her and she kisses him back, and then they both don't want to stop and surprise each other by going all the way.

"You must have done that with a lot of girls," she asks him afterwards. "Did I do all right?"

"You did fine," he says, feeling a bit of pride in having brought her along. "You're a great girl."

She assures him that she wants to go to every game and never miss the chance to see him play whenever he gets into the starting lineup or even if he only appears as a pinch hitter or runner. So now they are together whenever the Yankees play at home.

Ellie points to the gift-wrapped package under the table. "It's for you," she says to Conrad Thorp. "I had to go to a special store on Fifth Avenue to get these. They're really unique. Special, like you."

Connie opens the box and takes a bright yellow tube from it. "Why, it's shaving cream," he remarks.

"Not *any* shaving cream. It comes from California. Hand made in Mendocino from wild herbs that grow near the ocean. And it's got seaweed, too. It's all natural, very limited, made by one little family! Smell it!"

"It's incredible," he says.

"And look, look into the box," she urges him. "Not *just* shaving cream."

He takes out one item after another. There are at least a dozen.

"Aftershave lotion," he begins. "Body scrub. Deodorants. Moisturizer. Skin masque. Foot balm. You've bought the whole store!"

"The whole line, yes, I did," she admits. "Got it all. The salesgirl was so pleased. She said they have had it in for only a little while, and I was the very first person who bought everything possible."

"It's so nice of you."

"I'm awfully glad you're pleased," she says, clapping her hands, "because I read an article in *Good Housekeeping* that said men are too shy to go into a store and buy such things for themselves."

"I *am* impressed!" he says, and he turns her face up to his and kisses her.

"Tomorrow is the Fourth of July," Ellie says, "and you've got a night game. Let's celebrate at Rosa Mexicano's, it's just like the

136

restaurants on Western Avenue in L.A. I'll get dressed up fancy and you do the same. It'd be swell if you'd use these creams in the locker when the game is over. Use them all!"

He promises. They hurry away arm in arm.

Conrad understands the plot now. He has listened carefully. He knows what will happen.

On Independence Day Miguel Cairo comes up with a charley horse. Conrad Thorp gets to start the game.

In the fourth inning, on his second turn to bat, Conrad slugs a perfect standup double. He looks over the third base dugout, and there she is, waving. He's a happy man. He's going to stick in the Bigs, he feels.

At the beginning of the ninth, Ellie slips out her seat, waves goodbye to some of the female acquaintances she has made, and leaves the stadium. A block away she waits until the final out, then counts four minutes until all the players must be in the locker room.

She takes a cell phone from her purse and calmly dials the number that activates a switch in the box of fake, explosive all-natural lotions that Conrad is using in the locker room.

She hears the explosion. The entire Yankee team dissolves into bits and fragments of bone and flesh. She knows that the blast will burst through the stands above it and send chunks of reinforced concrete and steel whirling through the spectators still remaining there. George Steinbrenner will be among them.

The professor and the terrorist join her.

"Nothing matters more to the degenerate Americans than sports," the professor says. The Arab man adds, "What could be a better symbol than to slaughter the Yankees on the Fourth of July?"

On Independence Day, Conrad expectantly watches the last two innings of the Yankee game. No one named Conrad appears in the lineup. At the end, the only explosion comes when Joe Torre blows up at an interviewer. But Conrad turns on his laptop. A friendly tune greets him. He has a story to write. It comes easily. He thinks, terrorism is in. This is a *New Yorker* story sure.

BUDDHIST BASEBALL
An Autobiographical Fragment

You don't know about me unless you have read my *Journey to Heavenly Mountain*, which tells about the five months I spent as a Buddhist monk in the ancient monastery of Guo Qing on Mt. Tiantai, and about its abbot, Ke-Ming, and my best friends there, Chung-Miu and Fo Yuan, and its great master Qing Wai. I was the only one there who was not Chinese. Now, in my mind I am back there again.

It's 3:25 a.m. A half hour ago I got up for the first prayers of the day. I walk to the temple. Monks drift by me in their grey robes like quiet ghosts. I turn a corner. The temple appears out of the deep darkness. The fine old bronze incense burner is smoking and glowing. Candles flicker against the night.

I do what the others do. We bow and kneel, we chant and pray. The bells sound, the red drum murmurs. We sing as we walk around the temple, stepping in the footprints left by monks fifteen hundred years ago. Time stops here. Nothing ever happens at Guo Qing.

Five a.m. I am pacing the courtyard hoping that someone will step up and talk to me. I spy Qing Tai, the monastery's gardener. He often shows me a new bonsai that he is starting for the pleasure of Ke-Ming and the honor of Amitabha. But on this day he merely nods and speeds right by me, muttering, "What on earth!" and "I've never!" He's so overwrought he can't even finish a sentence. I pass through the place where the rice is boiled in a great pot and the vegetables are stir-fried in a wok so large a boat-oar is used to stir it. I quiz the cook, a reliable gossip. Does he know what's up? "Something strange," he says, and rolls his eyes. "What" I ask. "I don't know," he says. "Our delivery man, Li Fo, told me something, but it passed all understanding." A thing of wonder.

Chung-Miu is standing in the doorway of the dining hall. "What's happening?" he asks me, just as I am about to ask him the same. But Chung-Miu does know something. Li Fo had been down to Tiantai town early in the morning where he heard some news about what had occurred there the day before. But the story he told was so full of bewilderment that the astonished man couldn't tell what did happen. Maybe Ke-Ming knows?

Suddenly the courtyard before the temple is filled with sound. We hear it before we know what the hullabaloo is all about. We monks look at each other. Have the Red guards returned after all these years? Is

138

some other disaster awaiting us? At Guo Qing the old well-worn ways are so common that any new event seems momentous. I can see worried concerns wrinkling some usually placid faces.

Always ready to act, Chung-Miu stands up resolutely while the rest of us remain in wonderment. He looks out of the doorway. There he is transfixed. He is our champion of the day, and we crowd behind him to peek around his body to see what strange creatures have wandered into our peaceful haven.

Count them. One two three four five six seven. Seven Americans!

They are just nice college boys, big and blond mostly, with glorious curly hair such as my fellow monks have never seen. These boys are doing their best to be respectful and polite on the temple grounds, but they are full of burly merriment. It bewilders the monks. Somehow, after my long stay with the monks, I had gotten to think of them as the only sorts of fellows on earth. These seven Americans forced me to remember that these are the kinds of friends I had known all my life, boisterous guys who splash in the pool, poke each other in a jolly way, eat hamburgers and pizza at most meals, and pretend not to study hard, but get swell grades all the same. That they should suddenly materialize here surprises me, but at the same time I feel wholly at home with them. For the monks these Americans are as strange as a circus troop.

For the American boys nothing is impossible or outlandish. Whatever they are seeing in Guo Qing is what they expected. The world belongs to them. The monks never expected such a sight, however. They simply wait, holding their hands in the lotus position to see what wonders will occur.

My countrymen are astonished at only one thing – me! All at once, a tall fellow points at me and says: "Jesus Christ, look'd that – there's an American here!" They all looked. "Holy shit, you're right," another says.

"Sure I'm an American," I say. "What part of the country are you guys from?"

"From Oregon, we're all from Portland, God's country," one answers.

I explain this to the monks, except for the part about God's country, for the monks all know that God's country is China. I listen to their murmured replies. Then I tell the boys, "They want to know whether you have made your very perilous journey just in order to visit Guo Qing and to see its wonderful temples."

A fellow who seems like the spokesman for the group answers with a big smile.

"We didn't even know there was a monastery here until yesterday when we got to – what's the name of that town? – Tiantai." "But it sure is a swell place anyway," another adds.

I explain to my fellows, "He says that Guo Qing is famous all over the United States – even in their province of Oregon, and that they have spent many days traveling and yearning to see our renowned temples." A perfect translation. My monks like it.

"But now that you're here," I say, "surely you do want to see the temples?"

"Why not?" they say. We've come to see everything in China. Is it OK to take pictures?"

I tell the monks, "The Americans say that there is nothing to see in China more wonderful than our temples." When the monks hear this, they utter a little sigh of pleasure, preparing for the moment when the Americans will see such sights as they have never seen before – the treasured temples of the finest monastery in the world. One even clasps his hands to his heart in the universal gesture of ecstasy.

"Let me tell my monks your names," I say. "It's polite."

"Right. I'm Alexander," the spokesman says. He looks at the monks and does what he must have seen done in some movie, probably one about Africa. He points to his chest with both forefingers and says forcefully: "Alexander. Alexander. Alexander," with a big grin on his face.

"Ah-lux-ah-da," one monk repeats tonally. A Chinese name.

Alexander frowns a bit. But he graciously says, "Good. And this – pointing to each of his friends – is Larry. Bud, he's nicknamed after Budweiser beer. Davey. Jonathan – we call him Johnny. José. He wants to be called 'Jolting Joe.' Ivan, or Van. And Kareem." The Americans sort of stand at attention. "Now you," Alexander says to the group.

I sound out a symphony of Chinese names. Alexander doesn't try to pronounce any.

I hear hurried whispering behind me, but I can't catch its drift. Then I get it. "The monks want to know something else. Do you mind?" I asked the boys.

"Fire away," Davey answers.

"They wonder if you are really all Americans because you don't all look alike. Larry, they say doesn't look very much like José, and none

140

of the others look like Ivan. And obviously Kareem looks very different to them."

Kareem mugs with a heavy accent, "I 'spect dey think I'se from de Congo. 'Fat black buck in dey wine-barrel room'."

Alexander holds his arms out in a circle of inclusion. He nods his head vigorously and says: "All Americans." They understand his gesture. "Americans" they get. But what a strange miracle it is to them that no American looks like any other.

They study Kareem with absorbed interest. One of the monks is slowly reaching out one finger to touch the hair on his amazing skin. But he is still too shy.

I say, "Obviously you didn't come to China just to see Guo Qing. Why are you here?"

The incredible answer comes back with calm assurance. They are on a journey that will educate the Chinese and bring about lasting friendship between our country and China. Perhaps their mission might even signal the fall of Communism and the crumbling of The Great Wall. President Reagan, they believe, would be pleased.

"We're here to introduce China to baseball, or baseball to China," José says. For the seven boys, this is as inevitable as rain in Portland. Baseball is a good thing. The Chinese need good things that will bring them up to speed with the modern world – that is to say, with America – and therefore the Chinese must yearn to discover the mysteries of the American Game.

"Sure," Johnny adds, "All seven of us are on the team at Portland State. We applied for a grant to bum around China, and wherever we land, we find an empty field, lay out a diamond and play a game for all to see."

"Our idea," Ivan continues, "was simple, and the Goodwill Foundation brought it. There are about a billion Chinese – right? – and we know they'd always be plenty of them that would flock to the field to see how American baseball is played. Of course, we didn't suppose that all at once the Chinese would go nuts over the game and start forming leagues like the Japanese did. But we figured we'd make a start. 'One candle in the darkness.' That's a nifty phrase we used in our grant application. And we got the grant, so it must have been a good idea."

"How's it gone so far?" I ask.

"Great. Shanghai was a blast, we played lots of games there. Hangzhou too. We've just been working our way south, but soon we got to get back home. One or two more stops in Fujien, that'll be it."

141

I explain to the monks that the boys are bringing an American sport to China. The monks know about sport. They are intensely devoted to the Chinese national soccer team and to ping-pong.

Fo Yuan is the only monk at Guo Qing who speaks a little English. He was educated at the Buddhist College in Suzhou. He is a learned man, but intensely patriotic. I am not surprised to hear him speak up, "Yes, I see. We had such a game in China over five hundred years ago, but we gave it up as an inferior entertainment. Perhaps simple children or the rebels in Taiwan still play it."

I turn back to the team. "Baseball with only seven guys?" I query.

All the guys chip in to explain that in their game anything hit to the right of second base is an automatic out, and so they don't need a right or center fielder or a second baseman. Pitcher, catcher, first base, shortstop, third base, left fielder – that's six, and leaves one to bat. They rotate through the positions to bat, as if each man is his own team, three outs to a batter.

"What about runners?"

"Don't need'em," Johnny explains. "Grounder between second and third means singles. Man on first, imaginary runners. Another single. Imagine runners on first and second."

"It's line baseball, then," I say.

I gather the monks around me and using pebbles from the gravel path I draw a diamond with pebble players placed on it.

"We call these foul lines," I tell them. "It makes a baseball 'diamond'," I explain. I know the Chinese word for "diamond" only because of the great sutra.

Sure enough, Fo Yuan says for the approval of the congregation, "The Diamond Sutra has been chanted in China for more than a thousand years."

So these Yankees know the Diamond Sutra! The monks are impressed.

We give the team a little tour of Guo Qing. The boys are really nice about it, bringing forth the natural politeness which almost all Americans have. They make all the right gestures and exclamations of delight at each statue they see and each new room they visit.

When we finish the tour, Alexander says, "We want to show them how it's done."

"Done?" I don't make the connection.

"How baseball's done, of course. Our bats and gloves are in the van. And a box of baseballs. We always leave a bat and a ball wherever we

142

play a game so they can play it later themselves. Louisiana sluggers and real official balls of the American League. There must be a field somewhere on the property."

In the meantime our abbot Ke-Ming has walked out from his office and is listening kindly, without comprehending. I ask him if he has any objections to the team giving a demonstration. In all his years overseeing the management of the Guo Qing he has never faced such a query, but he takes it with the same calm equanimity that he always exhibits. I suppose that even if Buddha would step down from the altar some morning to pat Ke-Ming on his shaved head, he would still be calm. He nods yes to baseball.

A few guys run over in the van to assemble their equipment. I lead the rest past the buildings through a moongate, beyond which is a flat field. Quickly they pace out bases and a pitching mound and throw down canvas bases. Alexander Cartwright would have been proud of their measurements.

Larry is the first batter. Kareem's first pitch fools him and he taps a grounder back to the pitcher. A toss to first. One out.

The monks watch in silent wonder as the fielders whip the ball around the diamond to each other before tossing it back to Kareem.

"What skill," Chung-Miu whispers to me. "Just like the acrobats in Shanghai," he breathes in hushed tones. "Astonishing. Great masters. They must be national treasures in your Oregon."

Actually, these seven college kids are much better players than I had expected. They put on a good show. I can see they had developed a routine to make baseball attractive to Chinese. After a few batters, they form a chorus line in front of the spectators and do a rendition of "Take Me Out to the Ball Game" in barbershop harmony, at the end of which they bow and tip their caps in grand, fluid style.

By now other spectators have gathered – Qing Tai the gardener, Li Fo our truck driver, the gate keeper, my friend the cook, a delivery man, three nuns who are studying dharma at the temple, and even some of the farmers who grow our vegetables. There is a somber Taoist staying at the temple. I see him pick up a bat that is lying near the sidelines. Reverently he inspects it. Later, he also studies a baseball and a glove. Wood and leather – pieces of nature, vegetable and animal, living again through human use. Did this holy Taoist see some natural intimation of immortality in them?

To my surprise I see the old master Qing Wai walk slowly up to the crowd, watching with tired but determined eyes. Ke-Ming walks over to see if he needs a hand, but Qing Wai stands erect and steady despite his great age.

Every little while, the boys interrupt the game to explain something about the National Pastime. "Picture a runner on second base. You can't see him, but he's there. We don't have enough players to run bases too. So, if Ivan is at bat and he hits a double, that's two bases, then the runner on second will come home and Ivan has a score to his credit. Do you get it?"

I am translating as fast as I can, but the way it comes out is pretty confusing, and they don't get it.

"See," Alexander says. "It's simple arithmetic. Ivan makes a two-base hit. There's like, an invisible Ivan on second base. So if he hits another double, that's two plus two which means a man comes home."

The monks look at me in despair. "Home?" What does that mean? I point to the plate that the boys laid down and translate it as "end of journey." I say, "Ivan arrives at the end of journey and gets a reward." Now the monks get it. Invisible Ivan comes to the end of life's road, meaning, he's dead. In Homeland, Nirvana, with Buddha. Good. But of course, Ivan is standing before them, robust and alive. They understand this easily. Baseball is about past lives. A wonderful ceremony of the Diamond Sutra.

The boys enjoy instructing the monks in baseball. The monks are enjoying the amazing acrobatics of catching and batting and running around the diamond of life. They have never been witness to such surprising revelations that there is a Buddhist ceremony like this in America. Everyone is really pleased. This is when I see one young monk sidle over to Kareem playing first base and stand by him raptly until finally he reaches out and gently caresses Kareem's downy arm. Kareem doesn't mind. He smiles benevolently.

Eventually, the game comes to its conclusion. All seven players have batted. José has won with six runs. In triumph, he raises both arms, giving the double victory sign to show the monks that he is the winner. They bob their heads at him. One young monk imitates the Nixon gesture, then hides his face in his hands.

"Won't someone try?" Alexander asks, holding out a bat to the crowd. I translate the offer, but no one replies. To ask a Chinese to bat a ball would be as completely against nature as to expect an American to eat with chopsticks. They accept that I can use chopsticks only because they have concluded that I was a monk at Guo Qing in some past century. Otherwise, why would I have known how to come there?

"What about you, then?" He holds the bat towards me.

"Sure I say. Didn't I play on the Brooklyn Pioneers?"

I go up to home plate. Alexander delivers a slow pitch. Ah, no skill is ever entirely forgotten. I hit a soft fly over the shortstop's head.

Now my fellow monks are truly surprised. Dressed in his robes, Jay is still an acrobat. He knows how to do it. Chung-Miu gives me a big grin. Fo Yuan says that I must have been a baseball player in ancient China when they played this game. Past lives are never wholly forgotten, he implies.

Chung-Miu decides to try. He's in his early thirties and moves like a natural athlete. Alexander comes up close and pitches underhand to him. Sure enough Chung-Miu connects on the third pitch. The ball spins forward about three feet, but that is enough. The Chinese are learning baseball. Everyone is pleased.

That's the climax – of the baseball game. The seven wonders shake hands with everyone, even with Qing Wai. I stand by him to make sure he doesn't totter. They present Ke-Ming with a baseball and bat. Kareem comes over to me and asks, "Say, how did you arrange to stay here? I'd sure like to do what you are doing and be a monk. Maybe you could trade me in a one-player swap. Me for Chung-Miu, eh? Or for you. I'm really serious. I'd like to come." I tell him how to reach me back in the states. "Contact me, and I'll help you find your way back to Guo Qing," I say. I think he will do it.

The Americans leave, waving their goodbyes.

The field returns to the possession of the temple. It is a Buddhist field once more. The American players take all their noisy happiness and we monks return to silence. Some monks begin to drift back towards the temple. Others remain to stay near their beloved old master.

I tell Qing Wai, "Let me walk beside you back to your room. Perhaps you might take my arm. We'll go together."

"Wait," he says.

He has a faraway look. Perhaps he is thinking some very old thought, or maybe an entirely new one.

I wait.

Five minutes later he says, "Now, Yes. Walk with me. Let me put my hand on your shoulder to keep me steady. Help me back. I'm truly tired now."

I take him back to his quarters. On the way back, Qing Wai tells me, "Baseball is a profound ceremony. We all walk the wheel of life, always circling around the blessed giver of life, until we go home. My whole understanding of the world is enlarged today. Everyday, everywhere, everyone, even these brave, fresh, newly created American men, are singing their baseball song on their way to the Pure Land, even if they have no awareness of what they are doing. No matter. Neither do many of the poor illiterate monks at Guo Qing know what path they are following. They simply follow it."

Back in my own room I think long about this day's strange visitation. When darkness comes I realize I have missed evening prayers and it is already time for sleep.

At three a.m. I hear bamboo sticks beaten to rouse us to morning prayer. We will return to our routine.

But for me there is an even greater surprise to come.

When I reach the courtyard, no friendly incense burner glows to greet me. Darkness rules in the doorway too. No electric lanterns flash warm red signals to me. When I reach the temple door it is locked. I rattle the chain, but it refuses to yield.

Behind me my kindest friend, Chung-Miu, says, "You didn't come to evening prayers, or you would know."

"What?"

"Follow me.'

As we go I start to hear low chanting. We pass through the moongate. Specks of light dart from incense chargers. Candles cast wavering shadows on the ground.

It's yesterday's baseball field we are nearing. The monks walk in a circle just where the basepaths were, singing the Diamond Sutra, recalling Lord Buddha's wisdom. Chung-Miu and I fall in step at the end of the line. Where the pitcher's mound had been there stands a small Buddha. A lamp burns before him. A night bird flutters about the light. On Buddha's upturned palm is the baseball presented to Ke-Ming.

"Qing Wai explained to us all last night the hidden meaning of the ritual that your countrymen offered to us," Chung-Miu says. "And Ke-Ming agreed with his profound interpretation. He ventured to say that eons ago perhaps these same Americans were a band of holy Bodhisattvas wandering in the world, spreading enlightenment. Fo Yuan said that this old Chinese ceremony that you call baseball might have been played by the first holy ones in ancient days." 'Everything that is, is holy,' Qing Wai had said then. 'We are all on our way to the Pure Land.' So we decided to walk the path of the Americans today."

I see the visiting Taoist walking toward me. That seems strange at first. Then I realize that he is simply circling the basepaths in the opposite direction. True to his principles, the path we follow could not be his path. "Tao that is Tao is not Tao," Lao Tzu says. Always paradox. But he too, I knew, would reach his destination.

We walk and sing.

Our voices drift up to the sky with the blossoming smoke of the incense. Not far above us the smoke is whipped upward by the morning breeze. Our chant rises too and is swept away. The smoke and prayers rise beyond human sight and hearing.

ABOUT THE AUTHOR

Jay Martin is the author of twenty-two books involving literary criticism, psychoanalysis, biography, and autobiographical romances. He has also written two plays, one starring Glenn Close, John Lithgow, Colleen Dewhurst, and Tennessee Williams. His forthcoming book is a biography of Alexander Joy Cartwright, the "Father of Modern Baseball," and he is an authority on the history of baseball in Hawaii. He has taught at Yale, the California College of Medicine, the University of California, USC, and is now the Edward S. Gould Professor of Humanities and Government at Claremont McKenna College and a psychoanalyst in private practice.